MOTOCROSS BROTHER

by

ERIC HADO

Scobre Press Corporation
2255 Calle Clara
La Jolla, CA 92037

Scobre Press books may be purchased for
educational, business or sales promotional use.

Edited by Helen Glenn Court
Illustrated by Bill Wiist
Cover Design by Michael Lynch

ISBN 1-933423-81-1

HOME RUN EDITION

www.scobre.com

CHAPTER ONE

NO ESCAPE

The rocky ground below wrecked my bike. My head didn't fare much better. I ended up with ten stitches and a permanent funny-looking bald spot. I also ended up spending two hundred dollars to fix my bike. If I had to do it all over again, I'd still take the bet. I'd just be sure to dodge the pointy rocks.

Months later, I got the chance to try again. It was a hot day in the middle of June. This day was special because it was the last day of school. Eighth grade was finally over. I couldn't have been more excited. I was thirteen years old and looking forward to a summer of lazy days.

I sat on my bike, looking across my front yard at my mother's dented Toyota. A wooden ramp rested against the front bumper. I was sure I could make it over the car. I had definitely jumped my bike farther and higher than this before. I knew that there wasn't much distance to pick up speed. But the downhill slope leading to the driveway would help me get major air. There was no sign of Mom, which was definitely a good thing. I had just finished being grounded for my last stunt.

I walked my bike up to the take-off point. "You can do it, Jason! Show these suckers how you fly," yelled Big Joe, my best friend.

I never did stunts without an audience. A group of neighborhood kids waited to see if I was going to crash. I let my arms hang down loose and shook them. Next, I took a few deep breaths, pretending I was gathering up my courage. I always gave my fans a show.

I strapped on my helmet. Then I started down across the front lawn, pedaling hard. As I approached the car, I clamped on the brakes and stopped. The crowd went crazy, yelling with disappointment.

"Jason," Joe called out, "if you can't do it, just forget about it." This got the crowd screaming louder. Big Joe was always there to pump everyone up. He knew how much I loved putting on a good show. As my sidekick and promoter, he was an important part of the experience.

I pedaled back up to the top of the hill. Then I took off. I started pedaling across the lawn. Just as I was about to hit the ramp I saw my mother. She appeared in the front window of my house. Her mouth dropped open when she saw me go airborne.

As I flew through the air, I pulled the bike up underneath me. I easily sailed over the car's roof. A second later, I landed with a thump. The crowd cheered. I circled around them, riding a wheelie and waving.

I loved doing stunts like this. They made me feel like I was somebody special. Other times in my life, I felt angry and alone. My father left when I was a baby. It had just been Mom and me ever since. My Mom is always on my case about something. When I did my stunts, though, everything felt okay. It was as if my problems didn't exist for a moment. But then, just as suddenly, they would reappear...

As I moved through the crowd, the front door of my house flew open. All my fans took off running. "Jason, get in this house right now!" My mother screamed in her loudest voice. "Are you trying to kill yourself? Are you crazy?"

"No. Gotta go, Mom!" Then I turned my back to her, pedaling fast in the opposite direction. I knew it was the wrong thing to do. I knew this would mean another punishment, but I just couldn't deal with her yet.

"Jason! Get back here!"

Mom kept yelling and I kept pedaling. Big Joe and I headed toward the Jensen Dairy Farm. Sweat covered our faces as we made our way up steep hills.

We lived in Woodland, California, a town about thirty minutes from Sacramento. The town was about average size for a suburb. I'd lived there for most of my life, but was born in Iowa.

About an hour later, Joe and I began to hear familiar noises. The sound was music to our ears and awoke our tired legs. We both started pedaling. Within minutes, we turned into Jensen's Dairy. This farm used to be known for the fresh milk their cows produced. Nowadays, it's better known for the awesome motocross track on the property. Races were held there weekly. I showed up every chance I could.

"They're racing today," I said to Joe.

"You think so, genius?" He spoke sarcastically.

We passed cows chewing on grass. Big Joe tried to run over a chicken. When it flew up and touched his face, Joe freaked out. He lost control and fell off his bike, landing in a pile of cow crap. It was awesome. I never laughed so hard in my life.

Five minutes later, we were among the trailers, trucks, and motorcycles at the track. The track was a giant oval with bumps, hills, jumps, and nasty turns. In this particular race, the riders were all over eighteen and the best riders around. I couldn't believe how awesome these guys were. The bikes they rode were amazing, too.

Joe and I headed toward the finish line—the best place to view the action. A chain link fence held back the spectators. In front of the finish line was a huge tabletop jump. The take-off ramp was a curved wall of dirt as high as a garage. At the top of the ramp, the dirt leveled out for about sixty feet. We stared as the riders sailed over the jump. I soon realized what a joke my jump over Mom's car was. Bike jumps are nothing compared to motocross jumps.

Once they landed, they'd head down the straightaway to the finish line. My skin tingled with excitement as I watched. I imagined myself racing at the front of the pack of riders. I imagined kicking dirt back at the competition. *Someday,* I thought.

When I was younger, I always tried to convince Mom to buy me a motorcycle. Her answer included three no's: no money, no time, no way. Eventually, I just stopped asking. Still, I would dream about riding around that track on a motocross bike. Something about the sport of motocross just spoke to me. I believed it was my destiny to be a pro some day. Yeah, I'd have to get on a motorcycle and practice first. I was sure it would all happen eventually—somehow.

I looked over at Big Joe. "You know, if I ever got the chance to ride—"

He cut me off. "I've heard this a hundred times, Jas. You'd be the fastest guy out there." He laughed. "Riding a motorcycle and riding your bike ain't the same thing."

"I know that. You don't think I know that?"

Joe and I spent the next few hours watching the races in silence. Finally, we hopped on our bikes and headed home. The screen door squeaked as I opened the back door. It was just after seven o'clock. From the look of things, Mom had already eaten dinner. I walked over to the fridge in search of food.

I noticed an airplane ticket sitting on the table. I picked it up. It was one-way—from Sacramento to Des Moines. My heart started to beat more quickly. My father lived outside of Des Moines. Thoughts of him made my blood boil. *Who's going to Iowa?* I wondered.

Just then, Mom walked in the room.

"Is there any food in this house?" I asked in a nasty voice.

"I left you a plate of lasagna in the fridge. Just pop it in the microwave for a minute." Mom crossed her arms, obviously still upset with me from earlier.

"Thanks." I walked toward the fridge, then blurted out, "Why are you going to Iowa?"

"I'm not." She paused before looking into my eyes. "You are. You're going to spend the summer with your father."

"Wrong!" I said, making a buzzing sound, as if she had given the wrong answer. "Try again, please, the bonus round is worth double." My comments were dripping with sarcasm. I popped the lasagna in the microwave. "I'm not going anywhere. Sorry you wasted your money on the ticket." I tossed it back onto the table.

"Yes, you are." The look on her face was determined.

I stared at her angrily. I wasn't going to Iowa.

Joe and I had plans to expand our stunt show. Plus, I wasn't going to live with my father for three months.

I tried to soften my tone and get on her good side. "I don't want to be around him, Mom. Can't you understand that? I'll pay you back for the ticket."

Mom knew how I felt about my father. She remembered the last time I'd seen him. Mom and I had traveled to Iowa five years earlier, when I was eight. The trip was awful. Iowa was awful, nothing but corn fields, hot dusty roads, and flies. Mom tried to make me hang out with my half-brother, John. John was only two years younger than me, but he barely spoke. He wouldn't move six inches from his mother's side the entire time. *What a total wimp! How can Mom expect me to spend my summer with him?*

The worst part was that John wasn't half as bad as my father. I was in Iowa for three days and he barely even looked at me. He seemed more interested in drinking beer. I left his house crying and haven't seen him since. Some father.

Mom used to make me talk to him on the telephone every week. I was mean to him when he called, though. Eventually, he stopped calling as much. Now he pretty much just calls on my birthday.

Mom passed the plane ticket back over to me. "Your brother is excited about you coming out. Your Dad's a different person now, Jas. You need him in your life. Whatever I'm doing for you isn't working. You're out of control. I can't do this alone anymore."

I saw the tears in her eyes and it made me feel pretty bad.

Then she went on about how much my father had changed. I heard about how he quit drinking and how he wanted me in his life. As I listened, I had mixed feelings. Part of me hated the guy. I blamed everything bad in my life on him.

Another part wanted to like him—to love him like a son should. But I couldn't. I didn't care if he wanted me back in his life. In my mind, my father was a no-good drunk. I wasn't going to spend my summer with him.

The microwave oven beeped, but I was no longer hungry. I asked Mom, "Why are you sending me there? Don't you love me?"

"Of course I love you. That's why I'm sending you. I'm tired of you getting into trouble. I'm tired of you being disrespectful. I'm tired of your lying. I told your father that I didn't know what to do with you anymore. He said he would take care of you for the summer. He said he owed it to you."

"He doesn't owe me a thing!" I screamed and slammed my bedroom door behind me.

Mom spoke to me from the other side of the door. "What did I say about slamming doors in this house?" I didn't answer. "You're too big for me, but you're not too big for George." At that moment, Lieutenant George O'Leary stormed into my room. George is the lame cop who has been dating Mom for about five years. He's always trying to fill in as my dad. I've been working for years to keep him away from Mom.

As he stood in the doorway, I smiled. I couldn't help myself. Last week, Joe and I snuck up to his police car. We emptied two cans of shaving cream into the front seat through an open window. Then we watched from behind a parked car. When George saw it, his face was priceless. Our sides hurt from laughing so hard.

Mom stood behind George, who was massive, well over six feet tall. "I have to work tomorrow, so George will take you to the airport." Mom always had to work. "I'm sorry, Jason."

"I'll see you in the morning," George said.

George and Mom left me alone in my room. My packed duffle bag was sitting on the bed. I looked through it and pulled out four pairs of pants that didn't fit anymore. I had grown almost three inches in the last year.

After a quick shower, I toweled off in front of the mirror. I saw that the shadow below my nose was getting darker. *Maybe it's time to get a razor and start shaving.* The old fat around my middle had faded away during my last growth spurt. I could see muscles on my arms, shoulders, and chest.

As I looked at myself, I understood why Mom was sending me away. I was starting to look like a man, but I wasn't acting like one. This thought was quickly replaced with a different one. *I'm a kid, so who cares? I'm not going to Iowa.*

I knew that all I had to do was miss the flight. Big Joe and I would go camping and all would be back to normal. I quickly sent Joe a text message: "meet me campgrounds 3:30."

At three o'clock in the morning I slowly opened my bedroom door. All was silent and dark. My door made one little creak. I tiptoed down the hallway to the front door. Very slowly, I turned the knob. As I stepped outside, a deep voice spoke from behind. "Going somewhere, Jason?"

I almost jumped out of my pants. George's voice scared the breath out of me. Only my toes touched the floor as I tried to run. George grabbed me and lifted me up by my belt. I wasn't going to meet Big Joe. I was going to Iowa.

CHAPTER TWO

IOWA

The next day, my father picked me up at the Des Moines airport. My half-brother John was there too. We all shook hands and talked awkwardly for a bit. Dad kept telling me how tall I had gotten. John didn't say much at all. It was really weird. Just what I had expected.

Dad tossed my stuff in the back of his pickup and we headed off. We drove in relative silence for about an hour. Occasionally, Dad would point out some stupid Iowa landmark.

We turned off the highway onto a side road.

"How much farther?" I moaned. This was the first thing I had said since the airport.

"About ten minutes," my father answered.

I stared out of the window as green corn fields rolled by. It was crowded and windy in the front of the truck. The three of us sat side by side, squished together uncomfortably. I realized why Dad had brought John along and pushed us close together. He thought this would help us become friends. I saw right through that plan. *Not happening, Pops.*

I looked at John, then at the sea of corn. "How can you even tell where you are?" I snapped. "There's nothing here but corn fields, and they all look the same." My father turned his head. He looked toward me but didn't say anything. John stared at me like I was stupid. I returned his dirty look.

What an awful place to waste the summer. I wonder what Big Joe is doing right now. How is he going to get by without me doing stunts? I reached in the pocket of my jeans and grabbed my cell phone. The signal icon indicated no service out here. A feeling of loneliness pressed down on me.

Dad turned left onto another country road. Off in the distance I saw signs of civilization. "Do you think we can stop at that burger place?" I asked. "I'm starving."

"Sure."

Bob's Burgers looked like any other fast food place. Every few seconds, a loud buzzing sound came from the french-fry machine. Then a woman would push the stop button, dump out the fries, and refill it.

As we stood in line, the fryer buzzed again. Dad gave our order. My mood had changed from angry to bored. I decided to let out a loud "buzz" like the french-fry timer. Responding to my noise, the woman dumped the basket of half-cooked fries, and reloaded it.

John began to laugh. Even though he wasn't going to be my friend, he was my audience.

The woman pushed the go button and moved to do something else. I gave another buzz. She turned around and pushed the stop, then the go button again. She looked confused. John was laughing really loud. I let out one more buzz as she turned away. John's laughter caught her ear this time. She looked at the timer and then back at me. "Very funny, boys. We're a little too busy for your jokes right now."

Dad gave me a stern look and a slight smile. I looked away from him when our eyes met but followed him to an open table. We sat down at a booth.

"So how's your mother?" Dad bit into his burger.

"Fine," I said, quickly shifting back to my angry voice. "Actually, she's tired."

"Is she sick or something?"

"No. She works two jobs all the time, so she's always tired." *No thanks to you*, I wanted to add, but I didn't want to have a fight my first day here. There was plenty of time for that. So my mouth stayed closed. Well, except for filling it with half-cooked fries.

Thirty minutes later, we stopped in front of a two-story wooden farm house. There wasn't anything fancy about it, just walls and a roof. Still, it was a pretty nice house. A large red barn stood off to the side. Through its open doors, I could see a large farm tractor.

I got out and looked around. No other buildings were in sight. The flat, dirt parking area extended into the green waves of corn. The corn seemed to go for miles in every direction. The house was like a desert island in an ocean of corn.

That lonely feeling pressed down on me again. *How could Mom do this to me? It's like being in prison here. I'm stuck in the middle of nowhere, with strangers!*

"Grab your bags, Jason," my father said. "John, show Jason to your room." I followed him through the front door. To the right were the dining room and the kitchen. On the left was a living room with a couch and a small TV. John walked up the stairs, then down a hallway that led to two bedrooms. The floorboards creaked with every step.

"You have the top bunk," John said, tossing one of my bags up. "I cleared out a few drawers for your stuff. Half the closet's yours, too."

"Thanks." I unzipped my bag and started to unpack. The room was so tiny. The bunk bed took up most of the space. A small dresser and desk took up the rest.

"What do you want to do now?" John hovered like a house fly.

"Nothing," I mumbled. "Can you just leave me alone for a minute?"

John nodded and walked out. He looked as if his feelings had been hurt. *Who cares.* I was frustrated at being stuck here with no way to get back home. I was also going to have to spend my entire summer hanging around John. *Aside from a father, what could we possibly have in common?*

Just as it crossed my mind, the question answered itself. Five pictures of motocross racers hung on the walls. *John likes motocross. Cool.* I started to look more closely around the tiny room. My eyes jumped to a pile of motocross magazines piled on the desk. Next to them were four model motorcycles. I opened the closet doors and saw two giant motocross posters. "Not bad, John," I said aloud.

Just as I closed the closet, the thump of car doors startled me. I looked out the small bedroom window and saw John's mother. Dad and John were helping her carry groceries into the house. I walked down the stairs toward the kitchen. I stood awkwardly in the doorway.

I watched as the three of them moved around, putting the food away. They were like a basketball team who had run through this drill a thousand times. They darted past each other to one cabinet or another.

"Jason," my father said, finally noticing that I was there. "You remember Ann, right?"

"Hello, Jason. How was your flight?"

"Okay," I mumbled, walking over to shake her

hand.

She pulled me close and gave me a hug. "We're so happy to have you here."

"Thank you." I was surprised by all the attention I was getting.

Dad could see I was uncomfortable. He glanced over and we stared at each other for a second. "John," he said, "take Jason outside and show him around."

I followed John out into the afternoon heat. We walked to the swimming pool. "This is the pool," he said. "Over there is the barn. On the side of the barn is a basketball court."

"And past the basketball court is the corn."

"Yeah, I guess you noticed that," John replied.

"You have a tractor in the barn?"

"Yeah, come on, I'll show you." Walking in from the sunlight, the barn was like a huge dark cavern. The green tractor's back wheels were tremendous, taller than me. I climbed four steps into the seat and took hold of the steering wheel. This was pretty cool.

"Dad lets me drive it sometimes."

"Back home, I drive backhoes," I lied.

"You drive a backhoe?"

"Sure. My buddy's father has a construction business. He lets us dig with his machines. His backhoe is like this tractor. The only difference is that the backhoe has a giant bucket arm to dig with." I felt more comfortable when I was telling lies.

"Wow, that's cool."

"We make a lot of money working for him." Lying seems to protect me somehow, maybe that's why I lie so often.

I sat on the tractor, looking around. The front of the barn was wide open with lots of space. The back half had a loft. It was filled with cubes of hay. Big, thick, wood posts and beams reached up to the roof. Beneath the loft were a bunch of stalls. It was too dark to see what was in them.

"What's back there?"

"That's where we keep the motorcycles." John sounded as if it were no big deal.

"Motorcycles?" I gasped. "Did you just say you keep motorcycles back there?" I jumped off the tractor. "Where?"

John flicked on a light switch, lighting up the first stall. Parked there was a clean, shiny, red Honda CR85. "Awesome!" I walked over to admire the bike more closely. "This bike is amazing. Is it new?"

John's voice was really proud. "Yeah, we just got it. We're gonna sell my old bike after we rebuild the engine."

"I watch motocross races all the time back home. It's my favorite sport," I told him.

"Mine, too. Only I don't watch. I race. See?" John pointed to the wall. Sitting on top of a low beam were about ten trophies. This was too much to believe. *Skinny little John races motocross, and wins trophies? What the heck are they putting in the corn out here?*

"This is my old bike," he said, pointing to the next stall. It looked the same as the other one, only dirtier. I sat on the bike, rolled the throttle, and pulled the levers. *Two bikes! This kid is lucky!*

Suddenly my smile disappeared. I climbed off the bike. John's perfect world was hitting me hard. If Mom and Dad hadn't gotten divorced, I would have had two motorcycles. I felt cheated and angry at the same time. I wanted to hit something. I quickly walked out of the barn.

"Where are you going?" called John. I needed to be alone. "Jason!" he called. "Do you want to take a ride?" I ignored him and kept walking. At the end of the driveway, I turned right and started running.

Twenty minutes later, I was tired and drenched in sweat. I stopped along what looked like a major road. The traffic was moving fast. To pass the time, I began counting the fancy cars. Four Porches and two Corvettes sped by during my hour on the roadside. They were awesome cars.

I wished that I could get one and drive myself back to California. *A Porsche or a Corvette—which would I rather have?* I wondered. It was a tough choice. Corvettes had the horsepower and the powerful American look. Porches had the smooth, fast lines of a European sports car.

"See any nice cars?"

I looked up, surprised to see my father. He sat

down next to me on the side of the road.

"A few Porches and Corvettes." I stood up.

Dad stood up as well, dusting himself off. "Which is your favorite, if you had to choose?" *What is this guy, a mind reader or something?*

"I dunno," I said, looking Dad right in the face. The crazy thing was that he and I looked exactly the same. That kind of bothered me. "How did you know I was looking for fancy cars?" I asked as we started walking back toward his pickup.

"I've been watching you for twenty minutes. You had to be doing something." He paused, opening the truck doors. We both hopped in. There was no point in trying to run away. Where was I going to run to? Dad stuck the key in the ignition. "I know being here isn't easy for you, but it'll get easier." He revved the engine. "How you doing so far?"

"I'm wonderful," I answered sarcastically.

"I bet," he said with just as much sarcasm. "I thought you might be feeling bad. Your mother sends you away to stay with a family you don't know. You must miss your home and friends." Dad cleared his throat. "I want you to know that I'm glad you're here with me. Thank you for coming and giving me another chance."

I looked up into his eyes. I'd never thought of this trip in that way. I never realized that my coming out here was giving *him* another chance. For a moment, I was glad that George forced me onto that plane.

"So which do you like better?" he asked again, "Porsche or Corvette?"

"Porsche."

"What model?"

"1987 Turbo Carrera, convertible, with a whale-tail spoiler."

"Color?"

"Black."

"Good choice. Let's go home."

CHAPTER THREE

MAKING A SPLASH

Two hours later, pool water sent a shock through me as I landed a cannonball. We'd just finished dinner and the heat of the day was fading.

"Wow, nice splash," said John.

"That's nothing. You should see the ones I do at home. We have an in-ground pool with a diving board. I can make a splash that sends water all the way back to the house." I lied again. We didn't have a pool.

"Really?" said John. He asked a lot of questions.

"Yeah," I answered, rolling my eyes. "The key to a big splash is height. You have to get up high."

"How high?"

"As high as you can. Watch this." I got out onto the pool deck and hopped up on the railing. I ran along the top of the railing toward the pool. I leaped into the air and tucked into a ball. The water stung as I landed. A moment later, I stood up to see the result.

"Oh, that was awesome!" John spoke with amazement. I smiled with pride. "That was huge!" he added.

I looked around and got another idea. "Not bad," I said, "but I can do better." There was a ladder leaning against the roof. I got out and began to climb up onto the roof.

"What are you doing?" John's voice was nervous.

"I'm going to make a real splash."

"You're going to kill yourself. Don't do it."

"Don't be a girl. It's only about ten feet from the roof to the edge of the pool. I can jump that, no problem." I always felt like I had to make people notice me. When I could make people *ooh* and *ah*, I felt great. This was just like back home. Bring on the next stunt! All I needed now was Big Joe drawing the crowd in.

"Don't do it, Jason. Dad will get really mad."

"Do you want to see a big splash or not?" I replied in an annoyed voice. I'd reached the top of the ladder and was walking along the roof. I took a deep breath and started my run. When I reached the edge, I jumped up and out. Running downhill made it difficult to jump high, so I traveled mostly out. I swung my arms and legs forward to help clear the pool's edge. Tucked into a ball, I missed the edge by inches and slammed against the water. My butt stung like I had been spanked. I tumbled forward and hit my knee and forehead on the pool's floor. This hurt a lot more than my butt did.

I came up holding my head to hear John laughing and cheering. I had to hand it to him—he had one contagious laugh. Once he started, I couldn't help laughing along with him.

"That was incredible!" he yelled. "The splash went across the whole pool like a wave!"

I smiled. It was fun splashing in his pool and impressing him. The fun didn't last long, though. The back door opened and out came Dad and Ann.

"What was that noise? What are you guys doing out here?"

"We're just swimming." Dad didn't say anything, he just looked around.

"What made that big noise against the house?" Ann asked again.

"The ball hit the house," I lied.

Dad looked up at the roof. I followed his eyes up and saw water dripping down. It was water that had run off my bathing suit while I was up there.

"Did you jump off the roof into the pool?" His eyes met mine again.

"No. I told you, the water's from the ball." Dad looked at John, then back at me. John stood in the water with his mouth open, not knowing what to say.

"All right, both of you get out of the pool," my

father barked. "Jason, take a minute and think about what just happened. Dry off, and then meet me in the barn with your tennis shoes on." I looked over at John. He was wasting no time climbing out of the pool. Then I thought about Dad and the barn. *What would he want to do with me in the barn? With tennis shoes?*

Ten minutes later, my father was waiting for me as I walked into the barn. "Come and sit down." He closed the barn doors behind me with a thud. I didn't flinch. He grabbed a lock from his pocket and walked toward the doors. He clamped the lock over the exit. Then he walked back and sat down. "You and me are gonna be in here until we figure this out, okay?"

I walked over and sat across from him. "You're going to lock me in here because I threw a ball at your house?" I didn't plan on admitting that I'd jumped off the roof.

Dad was average height and weight, but he was all muscle. Still, he didn't look scary or mean. I figured this would be like the usual talks from teachers or my mother. No big deal. "Do you know why I asked you to come in here, Jason?"

"You want to take me on a hay ride?" He didn't smile at my joke.

"Because when I talk to my children, it's only between us. It's nobody else's business. It's my way of showing you respect. Do you understand?" I just looked at him, my face blank.

"Sure, whatever." I was feeling angry again.

Whenever I get into trouble I get angry. It's like I'm being attacked or threatened, and I want to fight back. Even if I know I did something wrong.

"So, do you know why I want to have a talk with you?"

"Because you haven't seen me in five years. Now you want to catch up on things." I was being sarcastic again. This didn't bother him like I thought it would. His face showed no expression.

"I want you to stop lying. There is no reason to lie to family. We're on your side."

"I don't lie."

"Yes, you do." He spoke quietly. "You've been lying quite a bit, and you've only been here for one day. While you're in my house, I don't want you lying. For every lie, you're going to jump over this bale of hay fifty times. We saw how much you like to jump, so you should enjoy this." *This guy is nuts!* I thought. *No way was I going to do this. What did I look like, a rabbit?*

"Right, sure. You say jump, and I'm supposed to say how high, right? Forget it. I didn't lie—I'm not jumping." Dad didn't know who he was dealing with yet. I wasn't like Quiet John, who would do whatever he said. While he was in Iowa, I was living in California, on my own.

"I see," he said quietly. "I guess we're going to be in this barn for a while."

"I guess so."

For the next ten minutes, Dad just sat there. Meanwhile, I was starting to want out of the barn. Finally, I spoke. "So, we're really going to sit here all night?"

"That's up to you. What kind of backhoe did you drive for your friend's father? Was it a John Deere?"

"Yeah, that's right." I couldn't think of another kind of tractor, so I agreed.

"Show me on my tractor how to lift the front bucket."

I walked slowly over to the machine. I studied it carefully, trying to figure out which lever would lift the bucket. There were too many, so I guessed. "That one right there," I said, pointing to a group of them.

"Put your hand on it."

I picked one out and touched it.

"That one tips the bucket. It doesn't raise it up." Dad sighed. "I don't believe you ever drove a backhoe." He had me and we both knew it. "You lied about driving a backhoe. You lied about jumping off the roof."

I hung my head. This was a strange conversation for me. Usually, when Mom got mad at me, both of us were yelling and slamming doors. This was different. Dad spoke to me in a calm, but strong, voice. And he'd done all of this in a place where there was no escape. He looked at me in the eyes as he spoke and never seemed angry.

His style of parenting was more difficult than Mom's to deal with. When she started yelling, whatever I'd done wrong got lost in the chaos. I would just start yelling back and soon the anger took over. From there, we'd agree on a punishment but nothing would really be settled. This was different. There was only one way out of it: to admit my mistakes.

"So, what's the punishment? You got me, okay? I lied." I was sure that Dad was already getting sick of me. "I admit it!"

Instead of giving out a quick punishment, Dad smiled. "I'm glad you admitted it, Jason. That's really great. Now, the punishment is easy, fast and memorable——and then it'll be over. No hard feelings from either one of us. You must jump over this bale of hay fifty times for each lie you told. Are you ready?" he asked.

"Are you serious?"

"Yes. You jump and I'll count." I stood with my feet together, swung my arms and jumped over the bale. "One," he said. I had to lift my knees high to clear the hay. "Two." I jumped, and jumped, and jumped. My breathing was deep and hard. Sweat ran down my face, stinging my eyes. Somewhere around forty jumps I stopped counting. My legs turned to rubber and then to jelly. They barely worked at all.

Dad cheered me on like I was playing a sport. "Come on, Jason, you can do it! Jump! Hit it hard!" I couldn't make it over the bale on my last few tries. He caught me as my knees landed on the bale and I started to fall. Finally, he said I was finished. My shirt was soaked and sweat was pouring off my face. He unlocked the barn doors and we stepped outside. The fresh night air tasted refreshing. I stumbled towards the house, exhausted.

"So, manual or automatic?" he asked before we stepped into the house.

"What?"

"The black Porsche, would you buy it with a manual or an automatic transmission?"

I caught my breath and smiled. "Manual. Definitely."

CHAPTER FOUR

THE RIDE

The shower washed away the sweat, dirt, and hay. When I was finished, I stood staring at myself in the bathroom mirror. I was totally confused. Yesterday, I hated my father. Everything wrong in my life seemed to be his fault. But he was nice to me down by the highway. I had the feeling that he actually cared about me. I had never thought that he did.

Then he punished me in the barn, which was not cool. Yet, at the same time, it was. I had lied, and that was wrong, so I deserved it. Knowing that he wanted to teach me something, rather simply punish me, meant a lot. Plus, the punishment wasn't long and drawn out. Dad's approach was quick, sweaty, and finished—just like that. I'll never forget it.

Two hours later, I was lying in bed. The electric fan hummed on the desk. Every ten seconds cool air blew across me. The day's events were buzzing around in my head.

"John," I whispered. There was no answer. "John," I whispered again. I shook the bed and said his name a third time.

"Mmmmmm."

"Are you awake?"

"No," I heard from below.

"What's it like to race motocross?" I asked.

"Fun," he mumbled. "Go to sleep."

"That's it? Racing motorcycles must be more than that. Come on, what's it really like to race?"

"You can ride with me tomorrow and find out for yourself."

"Awesome!" I whispered.

"Do you know how to ride a motorcycle?"

"Sure," I said. This wasn't really a lie. I did know a lot about motorcycles. I knew how to ride from watching other people do it. I just hadn't actually gotten the chance to try it out myself yet. "Kind of," I added.

The next morning, I watched carefully as John started his motorcycle. First he reached down and turned on the gas. Then he pulled up on something under the gas tank. After two hard kicks on the starter, the motor ran. John sat on the motorcycle letting it warm up. Then he reached down under the gas tank again. The engine ran with a quick pup-pup-pup-pup sound. John put on his helmet and was gone out of the barn.

I felt a buzz of excitement running through me as John left. I was about to ride a motorcycle! Now I just had to figure out how to do it. After a look, I found a button labeled *choke,* and pulled it up. Then I swung out the kick-start lever and gave it a kick. My foot slid off, and my shin scraped across the foot peg. Arrows of pain shot up my leg. My jeans saved some of my skin, but not all of it.

On the fourth kick the engine came to life. I turned the throttle and heard the motor turn faster. The throttle was the right handlebar grip. It's like the gas pedal on a car. Twisting the grip feeds more gas into the engine and makes the bike go faster. The bike felt alive under me . . . then the engine stalled.

I kicked it again. Nothing happened. It wouldn't start. Five more quick kicks did nothing to awaken the motorcycle. I sat there and wondered if I had broken it.

John rode back into the barn. "What's the matter?"

"It stalled and it won't start," I confessed.

"Did you take the choke off?"

"Oh, yeah," I said, and pushed the button down.

"Open the throttle," he said, but I was too busy kicking to listen. He let me kick for a long time. My leg felt like it was ready to fall off.

"Open the throttle and hold it while you kick." On the third kick, the motor fired. On the fifth, it ran.

"Ready?"

"Yeah," I said.

He kicked his bike into gear and was gone again. I stepped on my shift lever expecting to follow him. Instead, the motorcycle leaped forward two feet and came to a sudden stop. My excitement turned into frustration and embarrassment. I tried to kick start it again. This time, the bike rolled forward while I kicked. It threw me off balance and I struggled to keep from falling. John rode back in the barn.

"What's the matter now?" John was clearly losing patience.

"It stopped and won't start. This bike is a piece of junk!" John shut down his bike and hopped off.

"Let me try it." John pushed the bike forward. It wouldn't move.

"See, it's broken. I knew it. This thing is junk. That's why you got a new one—" Brim, pup-pup-pup-pup. John looked at me and made the engine scream. The back tire spit dirt and the front wheel jumped into the air. He rode a wheelie out of the barn.

"Ugh!" I yelled as I kicked the side of the barn in frustration. I felt like a complete idiot. I was frustrated, embarrassed, and angry all at once.

I heard the motorcycle coming back fast. John raced in as I jumped out of the way. The bike came to a sudden stop right where I had been standing. The engine fell silent and we just looked at each other. He could tell I was angry.

"I don't think it's broken," he said quietly.

I just looked back at him. I wanted to ride so badly. I just didn't want to admit that I didn't know how. I had nothing to say.

"Want to try it again?" he asked. All I could do was walk away.

"Jason? Where are you going? Last night you were so excited to ride, and now you're leaving? Why?"

"Because I don't know how!" I yelled. "So shut up and leave me alone!"

"I can teach you. I mean, if you want me to." He had a confused look on his face. John didn't understand my anger.

"That would be great," I said. I suddenly felt like I wanted to hug him, but I didn't. "Hey, sorry I—"

John cut me off, starting his first lesson immediately. "This is the throttle. This lever in front of the left handlebar is the clutch lever—" I stood in front of the motorcycle and listened carefully as he explained everything. My anger and frustration faded away. I soon realized that a motorcycle was much more complex than I'd ever imagined.

John pointed to the chain running from the engine to the back wheel. "The chain turns the sprocket on the back wheel. The wheel turns, and the bike goes." I looked for the chain and sprockets. They were difficult to see in the dim light of the barn.

John saw my puzzled look. "Let's roll the bike into the sunlight so you can see better," he suggested.

In the daylight, I saw the chain and the sprocket mounted on the back wheel. "Got it."

John continued, "It's kind of like a mountain bike. Your legs are like the engine, they make the power that turns the pedals."

"Okay, but what's a gear box?" I took off my helmet. It was getting hot in the sun. I continued my search for a gear box.

John explained that a gear box is like the gears on a mountain bike. On a bicycle, gears make it easy or hard to pedal. First gear is easy to pedal, but you go slowly. You shift up to higher gears to go faster. The motorcycle does the same thing, but its gears are inside the engine. He pointed to the lower part of the motor. I moved around to get a better view. This was all starting to make sense to me.

"You change gears with this lever." John's toes lifted a lever in front of the left foot peg. "Hear the click? Each time I lift the shift lever, it changes to a higher gear. When I step down on it, I shift down a gear. First gear is all the way down, and fifth gear is five clicks up."

"Got it." I felt confident. When he compared the motorcycle to a bicycle, it all made sense. Next, he explained that between first and second gear is a half click called neutral. There's no gear connection there. The motor can run and the bike won't move.

You put the shift lever in neutral when you're starting the engine. That's what I was doing wrong a few minutes earlier.

"But what do I have to do to actually ride?" I felt myself getting excited again. It seemed simple when John explained it.

"Get on the bike," John said. I did.

As he spoke, I did everything he said. "First, you have to start the bike. If the motor is cold, pull up the choke button. If the engine is warmed up, keep the choke button down." I reached under the gas tank and touched the black button. "Second, lift the shift lever from first into neutral. Rock the bike. If it rolls, you're in neutral. See?" I rolled the bike forward a few feet. "Now, kick start the engine."

I reached behind my right foot and turned out a lever. Then I gave it a kick—the same way I had seen John do earlier. Beneath me, the engine came to life. My heart started to race. "Now, pull in the clutch lever and kick it into first gear," he said. And I did.

"Now comes the tricky part." This already seemed tricky, but I was more focused than I ever had been. "Let out the clutch slowly, and at the same time roll on some gas. It takes some practice. Once you're rolling, let the clutch out all the way and give it more gas."

"Okay," I said, trying it a few times and stalling. On my fourth attempt, I got it to work. "Yes!" I shouted. "I got it!"

"The lever on the right grip works the front brake," John said. "Also, the back brake is worked by the pedal on the right side."

After some practice, I was able to start the bike and ride. Riding that motorcycle was the most amazing thing. I had been searching for something forever, and I'd finally found it. I never wanted to get off. My face hurt from smiling so much.

After I learned to shift up into higher gears, I went really fast. The long driveway became a drag strip. We flew up it with the engines screaming in fifth gear. It felt like I was going a hundred miles an hour. I felt so alive. By the end of the day, I was convinced that I was born to race motocross. There was nothing else I wanted to do.

John was two steps in front of me as we walked back to the house. He was awesome that day. Teaching me the fundamentals of riding was the greatest gift. A bond was beginning to grow between us.

CHAPTER FIVE

MY FIRST RACE

The next two weeks passed by in a flash. John and I would wake up early each morning and ride all day long. John taught me everything he knew about motocross—which was quite a lot. We had a blast together. He and I had more in common than I had originally thought. I no longer disliked him for being the one who grew up with Dad. I accepted our situation for what it was—imperfect.

"Jason, your mother's on the phone," Ann called from the kitchen. I wasn't looking forward to this phone call. Dad told me that before I could race, I had to clear it with Mom.

"Hello," I said.

"Hi, Jason, how are you? What did you do today?" Mom always asked me this. I could tell by her voice that the question carried mixed emotions. On one hand, she missed me. On the other, she wanted to see what trouble I had found.

"I'm fine. John and I rode motorcycles again this morning. I really love it. And you'd be surprised—I'm not getting into any trouble. Not that there's much trouble to get in out here." I smiled.

"I'm glad to hear that. Tell me you haven't done anything crazy or dangerous." Mom spoke in her worried voice. I was sure she was about to tell me I couldn't race on Sunday.

"Nothing crazy at all, I promise. I'm really careful on the bike, Mom. I wear lots of safety equipment." I paused, clearing my throat before asking, "Is it okay if I race motocross this Sunday? There's this track here, and I've been practicing every day. Dad said I could race if it was okay with you."

"Jason, I don't know."

"John has been racing since he was eight and he's never broken any bones. Dad says I have natural ability and—"

"Yeah, but *I* know the way you are. He doesn't. You'll head right for the biggest jump to impress everyone."

"Please, Mom. You sent me out here for a reason, didn't you? Well, I've been here two weeks and I'm starting to understand why you did it. I really am." I paused. "You have to give me the chance to prove myself. This is the only thing I've ever loved doing. I'll be careful. Please." There was silence. "Please, just trust me this time." It usually takes about four *pleases* to win her over. "Please, Mom."

"All right, Jason, you can do it. But be careful!"

I was fired up. "You're the best, Mom. Thanks!"

"Okay, I'll talk to you tomorrow."

"I can race!" I said to Ann, hugging her. I ran outside and leaped into the pool. "I can race!"

Early that Sunday morning we headed off to the races. The truck was packed with riding gear, motorcycles, tools, and spare parts. The track was dug out of a piece of farm next to a small stream. It was a muddy path that twisted back and forth with jumps, turns, and hills. It was actually about a mile long.

John and I signed up for the Senior Mini class. Each class had riders who were the same age and had the same size bike. Every class runs two motos— which is an actual race. The combined score of the motos determines the winner of the race. In each moto, riders go around the track four times. It takes about three minutes to run a lap. Before racing, everyone gets the chance to ride three practice laps.

Once Dad parked the truck, John and I quickly suited up. I wore a hard plastic chest protector. My heavy pants held my thigh and hip pads in place. Shin guards also protected me. I looked like a soldier about to go to war.

As I walked alongside my bike, I wanted to scream, *look at me! I'm going to race!* It didn't matter that two hundred other people were also suited up. I was proud and anxious to get out on the track.

I looked around as John and I pushed our bikes toward the starting line. All around us were busy, excited people. A sharp smell of exhaust fumes drifted across the parking field. It grabbed my nose like hot red pepper on pizza grabs your tongue. It was the smell of power, speed, and excitement.

We joined the crowd behind the starting area. All of the riders from our mini class were lining up. I sat on my Honda next to John and we warmed up our motors. Vibrations from the motor passed from the handlebars into my body. After two weeks of riding all day, every day, I had become pretty comfortable on a motorcycle.

"Are you okay?" yelled Dad, trying to be heard over the sound of the motorcycles.

"Yeah," I yelled back. "I'm *real* okay."

"Take it slow. Learn the track. Don't race during practice."

I nodded. Minutes later, a man tapped my front fender with his flag and stepped aside. I gave the bike some gas and let out the clutch. The back wheel spun in the muddy dirt and the bike leaped forward. John was on my right side as we started, but he quickly moved ahead. After four seconds, we were at the first turn.

I was inches away from the turn when I realized that I couldn't make it. Panic flashed through me. *Go faster* was instantly replaced with *oh no!* My bike bounced and bucked. I stomped my right foot down on the rear brake, locking up the back tire. It skidded and slowed the bike. As I slid to the top of the turn, I dipped the handlebars to turn. The bike leaned, but it refused to go forward. During my stop, I had forgotten to pull the clutch, which stalled the motor.

The bike began to lean over. The other racers were passing me, or were already far ahead. I reached for the ground with my foot. But on the steep slope, the ground was too far below me. Over I went, down into the mud. I quickly found out that riding and racing were two very different experiences. I knew I was better than this—I just wasn't used to racing yet.

Unfortunately, things didn't go any better for me during the actual race. I couldn't do anything right. When I tried to go fast into the turns, I couldn't hold a smooth line. My front wheel would come up and my back wheel would stay in. This would force the bike sideways. The jumps weren't much better. Sometimes I took off and landed clean, and sometimes I didn't.

On a small double jump, I landed hard on my front wheel. The back of the bike rose up and flipped me over the handlebars. I did a face plant into the track and came up spitting dirt. Another time, I didn't land straight on a tabletop jump and rode off its side. It was steep like a cliff and I went over the bars again.

The only thing I could do right that day was go fast on the straight sections. That felt incredible. Although I wasn't a good rider yet, I had a natural feel for the bike. Feeling the power of the bike was worth all the bruises and scrapes. I would hoot and yell to myself as I got to top speed. This was my way of letting the fun burst out of me.

Late that afternoon, John and I sat behind the truck, relaxing. It had been a long, hot day. I felt tired, bruised, battered, and happy. "Want to go down and see how we finished?" he asked.

"Sure." We walked past the other cars, trailers, and trucks. Near the front was a huge new camper about the size of a bus. Hitched behind it was a trailer with a fancy paint job. It had a picture of a jumping motocross bike and large lettering. "Simpson Racing Team, #10, Steve Simpson."

"Wow, look at this," I said as we walked by. "These people must have money coming out of their noses."

"Yeah, they do. That's Steve Simpson's father. He owns a chain of auto parts stores."

"What class does Steve race in?"

"Same as us, minis. He was in the race today. Number ten, the blue Yamaha."

"Is he any good?"

"Not bad. He usually finishes in the middle of the pack." We kept walking past the trailer toward the front of the track.

"So where are you?" I asked, as I ran my finger down a sheet of paper.

John looked over the sheet as well. "Here, I got fourth."

"That's awesome. What about me?"

"You're twenty-seventh. Not bad for your first race."

"I thought I was last?"

I heard laughter behind me. As I turned to look, it stopped. A tall kid with red hair and a big belly stood there with his friend.

"You were," John whispered, trying not to embarrass me. "The other riders didn't finish the race, so you finished ahead of them."

"Last is last, loser," the red-head said with a laugh.

When I heard that, my heart started to race in my chest. *Who the heck was this guy?* I took a step toward him. I thought about smashing his head with a nearby piece of plywood. Instead, I took a deep breath and walked away. Today had been a great day and I didn't want to spoil it. Besides, there were two of them.

Dad was packing when we got back. We helped him roll the mud-covered bikes up into the pickup. "Who was that jerk with the red hair?" I asked John.

"Steve Simpson, the rich kid from the trailer."

I looked back across the track at him. "I have a feeling I'll be seeing him again."

Dad interrupted our conversation. "So, what do you think about racing now that you've done it?"

I quickly forgot about Steve Simpson. "It was really awesome! I have to work on my turns, and the jumps, and the starts. Other than that, I did great. With some luck, I might even win next time." Dad and John laughed. They both seemed to enjoy my joke.

"I've been thinking," Dad said. "If you guys cut the hay in the field, you could make a track there. Since I sold the cows, I think we can use an acre for riding. Make a sketch of how you want things to look, and we'll work on it."

"A track right in the back yard? That would be amazing!" The thought of this got me very excited. John and I bumped knuckles and talked about how to lay out the track. If I was going to beat Steve Simpson, I would have to get to work.

CHAPTER SIX

MEGA-FIGHT

The sun was particularly hot the day after the race. The heat in Iowa was something I hadn't really expected. John and I spent most of that day cooling off in the pool. It was simply too hot to ride our bikes. That afternoon, Ann asked us to come along with her to run some errands. We agreed because we knew there was air-conditioning at Mega-Mart.

Two men with detector-wands greeted us at the entrance to the store. Just before we stepped in, we heard an electronic voice, "Bong. You have activated the Mega-Mart security system. Please stop and an attendant will assist you." A mother with two kids stopped as the security guards approached her. As they carefully looked through her cart, we stepped into the store.

John and I agreed to meet Ann at the entrance in thirty minutes. After our agreement was made, we went off in a different direction. We wandered over to electronics and flipped through stacks of DVDs.

A kid wearing cowboy boots and a football t-shirt stood near us. His t-shirt was stretched tightly over his stomach. He held a football underneath his arm. I recognized the red hair from the track. It was Steve Simpson—the kid who'd laughed at me.

I was still angry at Steve, so I decided to have some fun with him. "Did you ever see that movie *The Longest Yard*?" I asked John.

"No. What's it about?"

"This football player goes to prison and gets together a team of inmates. They play football against the guards." I started laughing loud. "There's this huge prisoner in the movie. His brain is the size of a pea. He goes around saying, 'Duh, will you teach me to football?' It's hilarious because he's so big and stupid." I started speaking even louder, so that Steve would hear me. "He wears a football t-shirt and cowboy boots."

From the corner of my eye, I saw Simpson look at me. John seemed a little nervous.

"Duh, will you teach me football?" I laughed my best stupid laugh.

"You'd better shut your mouth," Simpson growled, staring at me. John looked really worried. I winked at him and turned back to Steve.

"Oh, look, there's a big football player with cowboy boots on. Hey, were you ever in the movies?" I asked Simpson.

"I said shut up!" he growled again, with a killer look on his face.

"Hey, could I have your autograph?"

"Jason, let's go," John said nervously.

"I'm just kidding around. He can handle it. He had plenty to say at the track." I looked right at him. "You remember what you said to me at the track, right?" I paused. "Duh, want to football?"

Faster than I had expected, Simpson threw a punch at my head. I ducked under it and stepped to the side. He swung again at my head. I ducked this punch too, and shifted to the other side. This time, I drove my fist into his belly. Beneath two inches of mushy fat was a wall of strong muscle. Although he didn't look it, Simpson was as solid as a rock. This had suddenly turned serious. I leaped back out of his reach into the aisle.

"John! Run!" I yelled as Simpson came at me. "Go!" I yelled again as John stood there, looking confused. I skipped to my right, behind a display stand filled with batteries. This was about to get ugly. As I had expected, Simpson's leather-soled boots were slippery on the smooth floor. The charging hulk slipped while trying to change direction and took down the display stand. Down he went with a crash. Hundreds of batteries rolled in all directions around him.

"You move around the store just like you move around the track," I said, laughing. "You're clumsy and all over the place."

He roared and threw aside the stand. Half a second later, he was on his feet coming after me again. It wasn't funny anymore. I ran down three aisles and turned right. He was only a few steps behind me. I heard him slide and crash into a display of paint cans. Another quick right brought me past the pet supplies. It was like a super-charged game of tag. He was fast, but I was faster. As long as I kept changing directions, I didn't think he could catch me.

There was a second entrance to the store and I ran for it. The automatic doors opened slowly as I ran outside. I dashed around the corner, hoping he hadn't seen me. Seconds later, I dared to peek around the corner.

Suddenly, Simpson was right in my face. His giant hand grabbed my shirt. His other hand pulled back into a fist. Fear seized me. This guy was big, and in the mood to fight. He yelled in my face. "Got any more jokes for me big mouth? I'm going to bust your face open!"

I tried to break loose from his grip. My hand clamped around his wrist and my other hand pressed against his thumb. I pushed on it as hard as I could. He howled in pain as I forced his thumb past its normal position. Slowly, he let go of my shirt. As long as I pushed his thumb, I was in control.

Simpson's knees buckled under him. "I'm gonna kill you!" he yelled. He swung a weak punch at me with his other hand. I dodged it, bending his thumb further.

"Listen! If I want to, I can break your thumb right now. But I won't. As far as I'm concerned, we're even. We can settle any score that needs to be settled out on the track." I hoped that came out sounding tough, though I was definitely scared.

Still, I had a problem and I knew it. When I let go of him, he'd come after me at full speed. I had an idea that I hoped would save me. I let go of his thumb, pushed him backwards, and ran past the store entrance. He jumped to his feet and gave chase.

I noticed two young security guards in the entrance area. The guards were barely working, they were busy chatting with girls. I passed right by them, looking over my shoulder. Simpson was running after me with a crazy look on his face. I ran to the far end of the building. In the middle of my attempted getaway, I spotted John.

"Be right back!" I said as I dashed by him. I was dodging shoppers as I ran back toward the other entrance. As I reached it, I saw Simpson about fifteen feet back. *Perfect*, I thought.

The two young guards had no idea what was happening. They were too into talking with the girls. I sprinted out of the building, trying to get lost among the shopping carts. From a few feet away, with my hands cupped to my mouth, I said, "Bong. You have activated the Mega-Mart security system. Please stop and an attendant will assist you."

Simpson came dashing through the doors just as I called out my fake alarm. The security guards jumped on him like he was going in for a touchdown. They took him to the ground and searched him. The girls looked on, very impressed. I ran back to the first entrance and arrived just as Ann got there.

"Ready to go?" she asked.

"Definitely," I answered, completely out of breath.

CHAPTER SEVEN

MOUSE CATCH

The next day, John and I stood staring at the tall grass in the field. John drove the tractor back and forth leaving a trail of cut grass. I looked at his sketch of the practice track and tried to imagine it. *Our own private track*, I thought. *Awesome.*

Two hours later, all the grass was cut. John and I hooked up another machine that raked the hay to one side. We'd have to wait an entire day before picking it all up. It first had to be completely dried out. So, with time to kill, we headed for the barn to work on the bikes. First we washed the motorcycles. Then we changed the gear box oil and oiled and adjusted the chains. We also cleaned out the air filters. Everything John did to his bike, I did to mine. It was a great learning experience.

During the afternoon, we spent hours stacking bales of hay in the barn. The hard part about this was that we had to climb up to the loft. It was about 10 degrees hotter up there—and it was about 100 degrees *outside*.

We worked quickly in the heat. The bales were difficult to lift up over my head, but I managed. Sweat rolled down my face and stung my eyes. It was the hardest work I had ever done. Still, I was having fun. Every time I felt tired, I peaked out at the soon-to-be motocross track. Then I got back to work.

As I picked up one of the last bales of hay, I jumped backward. A dead mouse sat staring at me in the face. Instead of dropping the bale, I lifted it high and stacked it. Then I grabbed the mouse by his tail.

A few feet away, John was putting down his bale. I called out to him. "Hey, John, catch!" Then I tossed him the mouse. He turned and automatically reached out for it. The moment it landed in his hands he leaped backwards into the stacks.

The look of horror and then disgust on John's face cracked me up. He instantly ran at me and knocked me over, punching my back and arms. I was laughing too hard to care. I tried to wrestle him down, but he was strong—and he was mad. Eventually, he quit throwing punches and laughed along with me.

By the time he tired out, we both leaned back against the stack of hay. We looked like scarecrows, with hay sticking to our clothes and hair. I looked over at John and laughed one last time. "You should have seen your face." In that moment, for the first time, I really felt like I had a brother.

"Let's go in the pool," John suggested.

"Great idea," I replied, hopping down from the loft. John followed me.

As we looked toward the pool, we both glanced at the hose. It was a moment when two people have the same idea at the same time. Thirsty, hose, water, drink, now! John got there first and reached for the nozzle, but I grabbed the hose away. I pointed the hose at my mouth and squeezed the lever. A mouth full of hot water was what I got.

After spitting out the water, I turned the hose on John. He yelled as he raised his hands to block the hot water. Streaks of dirt and bits of hay ran down his face and body. He retreated across the grass toward the pool ladder.

For the rest of that afternoon, we floated lazily on rafts. I was half asleep, tired, and happy. Thoughts bounced around in my head. Yesterday's race played over and over in short flashes. I relived each jump and every crash.

My mind then wandered from Iowa to California. A picture of my mother flashed in front of me. I suddenly felt the need to speak to her. Maybe I was homesick. Not that I would admit it, but I missed her. I rolled off the raft and climbed out of the pool. Then I grabbed the phone and punched in my mother's number.

"Hi, Mom."

"Jason," Mom paused. "Are you okay?"

"Yeah, I'm fine. I just wanted to say hi."

"Do you need money?"

Mom seemed surprised by the call. She reminded me that I didn't usually call her without a specific reason. But she was excited to hear from me. She said it made her day. I was glad.

I filled her in on every detail of the last few weeks. I told her about how much fun racing was. I also informed her that John and I were spending a lot of time together.

Toward the end of our conversation Mom took me by surprise. "You'll never guess where I'm going this weekend, Jason. George is taking me to a NASCAR race!"

"You and George—at a car race? Since when do you like racing?"

"I don't know. George loves NASCAR, so I figured I'd give it a try."

That's pretty cool. I never really thought George would be a race fan. I guess I'd never thought much about George at all. "I have to get back to work, Jason. Be careful on that motorcycle."

"Okay, Mom, I will. Bye." It sounds corny, but *nobody loves me like Mom* was the thought in my mind. I hopped back into the pool.

Once I was back on the raft, for the first time in a long time, I really thought about myself. I compared the way I acted at home, versus the way I was acting here. For some reason, my temper was calmer here, and I lied less. I was also nicer to Mom, and I didn't try to show off as much. I wasn't perfect, but I definitely felt different. I was happy. I owed a lot of that to motocross.

Since I started riding motorcycles, I felt a change. In California, it seemed like I was always angry. I was upset that my father wasn't around. I blamed his absence for everything. Now that I was getting to know him, that anger was melting away.

I started to feel bad about the way I had been treating Mom. She was my number one fan, and I had been giving her a hard time. I decided that when I got back to California, I would do things differently. A smile stretched across my face.

The next morning, John and I watched as Dad raked up the cut hay. He left some hay to help define the paths of the track. When John and I were finished loading the bales, we had a basic track run. There was still a bunch of work to be done to perfect it. We decided we'd done enough for the day, though. Once the track was clear, we hopped on our motorcycles and began to ride.

As John went through the turns, he cranked open his throttle. Dirt shot out from his rear tire. Each time he made a turn, the tire dug a rut. I tried to follow, but I just couldn't stay with him on the turns. His front tire always dug in, whereas mine would slide out from under me.

I skipped up three rows to get in front of him. My Honda tore across the track as I shifted up to fourth gear. I downshifted twice, slowing for the next turn. I stepped on the rear brake. John was right behind me. As I started to take the inside, he went to the outside. He was then instantly on the gas. As I rolled wide out of the turn, he flew past me. *Man, my little brother can ride!* Two rows later, he had stretched out a long lead again.

I began to get frustrated. *Why can't I ride like him?* Finally, I waved him over.

"How do you ride so fast?"

"I don't know. I just do it."

"Come on, John, help me out. I must be doing something different than you."

John took off his helmet and held it under his arm. "Go ride and I'll watch you," he said. So I did. I rode back and forth a few times around the track. I rode back over to him afterward.

"First thing, hit both brakes hard at the last second when coming into a turn. Hold on the front brake until you are about three-quarters of the way through. If you have the brake on, there will be extra weight on the front tire. That's how you get the front tire to bite into the dirt and not slide. That'll really help you. Also, move forward on the seat."

"That's all I have to do? Just slide up on the seat and hold the front brake on?"

"No."

"Then tell me more!"

"You have to work with the back brake and gas while turning. Early in the turn, roll on some gas. At the same time, pull the clutch while easing off the back brake. It all has to be smooth or it won't work. Make sure to downshift and watch out for the braking bumps."

I rolled my eyes. He was just making it more complicated. "What are braking bumps?" I asked.

"Those are the big bumps and holes that form right in front of the turns. They come from everyone hitting their brakes hard in the same spot."

"All right, let me see if I have this right," I raised my voice. John folded his arms as he sat on his motorcycle, listening. "I'm in a race with bikes in front of me, bikes behind me. After ripping down a straightaway, I hit my brakes as hard as I can. I'm also riding in and out of braking bumps. While I'm doing this, I decide on which path to take through the turn. I pick out the fastest line that won't allow the other racers to pass."

"Yeah, hit your brakes and pick your line. That's what I said." John smiled.

"Right," I said, returning his sarcasm. "So, I hold both brakes on as I enter the turn. I also pull in the clutch, down shift, sit down, and roll on some gas. I keep my weight forward and hold the front brake on. While I'm doing this, I begin to ease off the back brake and feed power." John nodded. "Now I'm half-way though the turn. The power is coming on, and I'm easing off the front brake. At three quarters, I'm off the front brake and on the gas."

I took a deep breath. This seemed like way too much to do during a race. I wasn't sure if I would be able to remember all of it.

John tried to reassure me. "You've got it. You're going to be fast."

"Is there anything else?" I was scared of the answer.

"Yeah, put your foot out in front of you in case you start to fall."

"How can I do anything else if I don't have my foot on the bike?"

John put his helmet back on and revved his engine. "Practice!" he shouted. "That's why we built the track!" With that, he rode off.

I sat on the seat of my bike, watching John for a while. "Practice," I whispered aloud. Then I went to the side of the track, riding slowly back and forth. Again and again, I did what John had told me. It was complicated, though, and I would constantly forget something.

Eventually, I decided to break down what he'd said into parts. First, I worked on using the back brake and feeding in the power. After that, I worked in using the front brake. It took a lot of attempts, but I started putting it all together. John had already gotten bored and gone into the house. I rode on the track for another hour or so.

I cruised around the turns slowly, concentrating on putting all the movements together. Down the straights, I went fast and set up carefully for the turns. Gradually, I was able to take the turns faster. My confidence began to build. My turning speed increased. I didn't do it as fast as John did, but I was getting better. *Just wait until next Sunday.*

CHAPTER EIGHT

WHY, DAD?

"This machine will drive through anything," my father explained as we stood alongside the tractor. "It's big, heavy, powerful, and dangerous, so pay attention."

"I understand." I was excited.

A few days ago, John and I stored all the grass he'd cut. Now Dad was going the teach me to drive the tractor. We were going to plow the field to loosen the dirt. Then we'd be able to easily move it and build jumps.

"A car has a gas pedal. A tractor has a throttle lever. It's right here on the side of the steering wheel. This is the gearshift lever. Down on the left is the clutch pedal. Those on the right side are the brake pedals."

I looked down and saw two pedals. I wondered why there were two. A car only has one. Dad read my mind.

"One is for each back wheel," he explained. "They help you make sharp turns. If you step on the left brake, the tractor will pivot on the stopped wheel. If you want to stop straight, step on both of them at the same time."

"Okay," I said.

"Get up in the seat, it's time to drive."

Dad stood on the steps right next to the seat. "Make sure the shift lever is in neutral, and turn the key." I moved the key and the engine cranked over. It ran with a deep, slow, growling noise. The tractor shook beneath me. "Give it a little more throttle," he shouted. "Now push in the clutch, put it in second, and let out the clutch slowly."

As I raised the clutch pedal, the big machine moved forward. I felt a sense of pride. I'd gotten it started, and I was driving a real tractor! I wished Big Joe and my mother were there to see me.

"Good. Head over there and we'll make a pass with the plow," Dad said.

The plow was a heavy rack of hooks that dug into the dirt. We drove slowly to the edge of the corn-field.

"Okay, lower the plow." I pushed the lever forward and the plow dug into the ground. The big engine roared in response to the heavy load. We rolled across the hay field, leaving a path of loose topsoil.

"When I say, raise the plow, go a little farther. You must turn the wheel hard while stepping on the right brake pedal." Dad had to yell over the sound of the engine to be heard. "Okay, raise it!" The plow came up. "Turn now!" I turned the wheel and stepped on the brake pedal. The big tractor spun around.

Very cool.

"Lower the plow and make another pass," Dad yelled.

Back and forth we went. It quickly became easy and my mind began to wander. I peeked at my father riding alongside me. It was great to have him teach me to drive and let me race. Whenever I was doing something with him, I felt that he liked me. I also felt close to him.

Still, it was easy to like him here. For years, though, I had thought he was a bad guy. *Who was he really? The father who didn't care? Or the father trying to make up for lost time?* This question left me confused. Something that I had believed for most of my life no longer seemed true. *Maybe Dad really is a good guy.* On one hand, this was a good feeling. My father was back in my life. On the other hand, I still didn't understand why he'd left Mom and me.

I'd been lying awake in bed thinking about this each night. Now, after being here a few weeks, it had surfaced again. I could no longer ignore it. "Why did you leave us?" I asked, suddenly.

Dad turned his head in surprise. "Stop the tractor," he said. I stepped on the brakes and clutch. "Turn off the engine, too." It suddenly got very quiet. "It's not an easy thing to explain." He looked off, avoiding my eyes. "You have to understand something. I want what's best for you. I always have. You're my son and I love you."

"So why—"

"I left because things weren't right between your mother and me. I think we both knew they never would be." He looked at me for a second and then looked away. "Your mom and I got married young. We didn't really know each other that well. After living together, we realized that we had differences—differences we couldn't overcome."

"So you left because you were different? Everybody's different. That doesn't make sense." I was really trying to understand what he was trying to say. I wanted to believe he had a good reason, I just wasn't seeing it yet. This "differences" excuse didn't connect with what my mother had told me.

"Your mom and I both grew up around Hudson. She didn't get along with her family real well. After high school, she couldn't wait to move out. Right after we graduated, we got married and moved away. The excitement of leaving Iowa wore off pretty quick. It wasn't as wonderful as we thought it would be." He continued. "After a year, you were born. Then my father got sick. My mother was home alone with him and the farm. The bank was after them to pay money they owed."

"I wanted to move back here to help my parents. Your mother understood that I was torn. At the same time, she didn't want to come back to Iowa. When I left California, I planned on coming back. But things happened that made that hard."

"Like your drinking?" I asked.

He stared into my eyes with a sad look. "Yes, that was part of it. I had a problem with alcohol and it took me some time to realize it." His lip shook a bit as he spoke. "I'm sorry that my problem affected you, Jason. I really am. But that's in the past now."

"Why didn't you come and see me?" I asked.

"When you were little, I did. It was expensive to fly to California, but I came as often as I could. As you got older, though, it got harder. Whenever I told you I was coming out, you told me not to. You ran away the last time I came, remember?"

I did remember. He wasn't the perfect Dad, but I wasn't much of a son either. "Can we start over?" I asked him, trying to hold back tears. "I mean, can we just start right here, right now?"

"That's all I want." Dad reached out and we hugged for the first time. That moment is frozen in my mind. We pulled back and sat in silence, watching the orange sun drop behind the corn. I was starting to see why Dad loved Iowa so much. There was something special about this farm.

CHAPTER NINE

JUMPS

I finished plowing the field to break up the hard-packed ground. Then John and I dug out the track, using the loose dirt to build jumps.

To test out our biggest jump, John took a quick practice run. He whipped his Honda around a turn, straightened out, and hit the ramp. Then he shot high into the air before dropping down beyond the landing ramp. He rode over to me as I sat on the big tractor. "We need a longer ramp on that jump," he said.

"Okay." I drove the tractor to the pile of extra dirt. The machine responded to my controls, scooping up a huge bucket full. I tipped the bucket above the landing ramp while John directed me.

After we molded the dirt, John was set to give the jump another try. He showed me the thumbs up after a perfect landing. I couldn't wait to try it out myself.

Without delay, I parked the tractor, and kicked over the Honda. I sped up to the ramp, and got ready for some big air. My back tire was still driving forward as it launched me off the ramp. A thrill of excitement flashed through me. An instant later, that excitement turned to fear.

The front of the motorcycle began to dip too far down. I thought I was going to go over the handle-bars, face first. I hung helplessly in the air as the front wheel crept under me.

The front wheel hit the ground first. My momentum forced my elbows to bend. I slammed down against the red gas tank. For a long second, the front wheel rolled beneath me. At last, the back end dropped down. It hit the ground and I breathed a sigh of relief. I missed the next turn and rolled off the track. Sweat poured off me as I sat on the bike trying to calm myself. I couldn't understand what had just happened.

John rolled up beside me. We both turned off our bikes. "That was crazy-close, bro. Take it easy on those ramps until you really know how to jump," John said.

His remark annoyed me. "I've jumped my bike hundreds of times, over cars and every thing," I replied.

"Oh. Okay."

"Don't just say okay!" I lowered my voice. "Just tell me what I did wrong."

"I didn't see it. Go crash again so I can watch." He laughed and I gave him a shove.

"Let's skip the crashing part. Go right to where you tell me how to do it."

John wasted no time getting into it. I realized that my brother was a great teacher. He said that teaching was his plan if he couldn't be a professional motocross racer. It actually made a lot of sense.

When John spoke, I listened. "There are a few ways to jump," he began. "As you approach the ramp, you want to be riding straight ahead. Stand on the pegs, and cut the throttle before your front wheel leaves the ramp. Keep your knees bent and squeeze the motorcycle with your ankles while airborne."

"Why do I have to squeeze it?"

"So it doesn't fall away from you when you're in the air. And, remember, start off slow. You're a beginner."

I practiced doing what John told me for the rest of the afternoon. I realized that the key was staying in control, not going for the most air. I was getting better at it, too.

Sunday came along with cool and cloudy skies. Dad, John, and I left for the races early. We parked a few spots away from the Simpson's huge trailer.

"Nice car," Simpson said, laughing at Dad's truck.

"Just ignore him," Dad said.

That was easier said than done. I opened the passenger door and stared over at Simpson. "Nice face," I said. John cracked up.

Dad wasn't laughing. "What did I just say to you, Jason?"

"Sorry." There was just something about Dad's voice I responded to.

The three of us walked toward the track. "Check out that new back straightaway and triple step-up jump," John said. He was staring at the new additions to the track. "They just finished putting those up yesterday."

I looked toward the new stretch of track—and the big triple. "Awesome." That jump was huge! Giant steps had been cut into the side of the hill. A huge take-off ramp would send the riders high into the air. It looked like fun, but if you fell, it would be ugly.

We signed up to race, and then walked around the track. As we walked, I tried to memorize all the new turns and jumps. After following the twisting path, we came up to the triple jump. "Look at the size of that take-off ramp!" I said. "It must be twelve or fifteen feet high. It's so steep you can't climb it on foot."

"Yeah," said John, as we climbed the steep hill beside the jump. His eyes were focused on the ramp. "The ramp is going to look like a big dirt wall," he said.

"Yup," I agreed, "a dirt wall that will wreck your

bike and your head." I looked across the track to the finish line. Last week, I hadn't jumped very far. On the first lap I had almost fallen. After that, I slowed down each time I approached the big jump. After practicing on our track, I was confident I could do better. This jump was huge—but I was ready for it.

Dad was back at the truck, unloading the bikes and checking them. After he finished, I changed into my racing gear. Then I went to work, getting my bike ready to race.

"Did you check the chain tension?" Dad asked.

"Yup."

"Did you oil it?"

"Yup."

"Check the coolant level?"

"It's good."

"Gas?"

"Full tank. And I checked for loose nuts and tire pressure. Plus, I checked the clutch and brake lever end play. I also vented the front forks, and checked the spark plug."

Dad raised his eyebrows, obviously impressed. "Good, now all I have to do is get your brother to do the same." I could tell that Dad was proud of how quickly I was learning.

Twenty minutes later, John and I rolled our bikes towards the starting area. As we passed the Simpson trailer, I saw Steve sitting on his blue Yamaha. His racing pants and boots looked brand new. He was staring at me as he extended his middle finger. He was obviously still mad about the incident at the Mega-Mart.

I took Dad's advice and ignored him. It was hard, though, because at the starting line, Simpson was there again. He lined up a few bikes to my left.

John was next to me as we warmed up our bikes. "Stay away from him, Jas."

I smiled at John as the flagman gave us the go. Off we went. I felt much more confident around the turns this time. My practice had paid off. I was able to ride faster through the turns. This enabled me to carry more speed into the jumps.

The back straight was a blast. I held the throttle wide open and banged through the gears. At the end of it was the giant take-off ramp. It was just plain scary. John was right about the ramp appearing as a big dirt wall.

On my first lap, I put on the brakes at the bottom of the ramp. This threw off my balance and I landed nose down. This was a safe move, though it slowed me down quite a bit. Because I wasn't going fast, it was easier to keep from falling. All of the more experienced riders cruised past me.

During the next lap, I didn't get so crazy on the straightaway. I approached the dirt wall slower, and more under control. This worked much better and I landed on the first step. On my third try, my brain began to overcome its fear of walls. I carried more speed and landed on the second step. Fun had fought its way past fear.

After three practice laps, the flagman waved his checkered flag. I followed the other riders off the track. Back at the truck, I got to work preparing my motorcycle for the first moto. I glanced over at Simpson, who was leaning against the side of his trailer. His father was working on his bike. Steve wasn't even watching.

Forty minutes later, I was lined up in front of the starting gate. John was next to me on my right. Dad was a few feet away, watching over us both. Five gates to my left was Simpson. I desperately wanted to beat that kid.

"Listen," Dad yelled. "Concentrate on the corners. Try to take the inside line. Have fun." I only half heard him. The excitement of starting the race bounced around inside of me. I nodded and put on my goggles.

The track starter stood on the far side of the starting area. He turned his signboard sideways, signaling that we were ready to go. In a few seconds, the gates would drop. I pulled in the clutch and toed the shift lever into second gear. My eyes were glued to the starting gate.

Suddenly, it twitched and I dumped the clutch. The back wheel spun, spitting dirt into the air. I hung on as the bike leaped forward. A full second later, I snatched up to third gear and roared onward. John was in front of me as the other motorcycles closed in. The engines silenced for a moment as the riders hit their brakes. I held my breath and tried to avoid the bikes packed in around me. We squeezed through the first turn and were back on the gas. The first jump was next. Riders leaped over the small tabletop jump in threes and fours. We looked like frogs hopping for the safety of a pond.

Blood pounded though my veins. It was a wild ride. I held the bars as tightly as I could. There was no time to think. All I could do was hold my position, riding the inside line through the turns. The faster riders went around me on the turns. John was well up in front of me. As the crowd thinned, I began to settle down. *Make a smooth transition from brakes to gas in the turns*, I thought. *Approach the jump straight on, cut the throttle before the front wheel launches.*

Everything seemed to be working for me. I was somewhere near the middle of the pack, running smooth and fast. We were approaching the big triple. I tracked perfectly around the fast left-hand turn. I held the throttle wide open on the short straight. Then I got on the brakes hard, as I downshifted. I could hear a motor very close behind me.

As I came out of the turn, I looked over my shoulder. I noticed a blue bike and a black helmet. Number ten. Steve Simpson was right behind me! *I can't let him pass me! Don't let him get by, Jason,* I told myself.

I cranked on the throttle coming out of the turn. I got a little loose in the back end. Simpson came out smooth and fast. He caught up to me as I straightened out. At this point, it was clear that he and I were racing one another. It was a drag race down the long straight with the dirt wall growing larger. The big brown monster was waiting for us.

I was torn. My brain said slow down and stay under control. My emotions, though, wouldn't let me hear it. I couldn't allow Simpson to pass me. It didn't matter if I crashed. I was living in the moment. Just as we got to the ramp, Steve hit his brakes. *Ha, I won,* was the only thought that flashed through my mind. This was immediately followed by *quick, hit the brakes!* I snapped the throttle closed as my fingers reached for the front brake lever.

The brown monster flicked me up into the sky. I hit my brakes too late. I was already into the air. I soared high above the first step and fear exploded inside of me. I was going to land on the *third* step. This was far beyond what I had done in practice. I was going to crash!

As I began to drop, the motorcycle was rotating beneath me. This was exactly what had happened on the farm. If I landed nose down at *this* speed it would be hospital time. Panic bit into me. I held on tight and backed up on the seat. As I did that, my hand rolled the throttle wide open. The engine screamed as my tire gripped nothing but air. I screamed along with it.

I flew beyond the third step, farther than I had seen anybody else travel. Just before I hit the ground, a miracle occurred. The motorcycle rotated the other way, lifting the front. The front wheel hit with the back wheel immediately following. I thumped down onto the seat, but I kept the bike upright. Somehow, I landed without crashing.

The panic disappeared and was replaced by joy. I screamed and celebrated my survival. I rolled through the first half of the big sweeping turn. The wide turn led to a tabletop jump. I cleared it and raced downhill. The rest of the race went by in a flash. Simpson didn't catch me. The checkered flag waved and I rode through the exit gate. I felt drained, out of breath, thirsty, and hot.

I looked back and saw some riders following me off the track. *I'm not last this time.* I watched Simpson roll past. He never looked at me. Dad gave me a high-five and John and I bumped knuckles. Ann was there to hand me a bottle of cold water. It felt great having that support.

The race was over, but the motorcycle continued to vibrate beneath me. I had survived the brown monster and beat Simpson. My body and mind were still tingling from the excitement of the race. I was totally happy. I wanted it to last forever.

CHAPTER TEN

BLOCK-PASS

"How did you do?" I asked John.

"Okay. I think I took fourth, how about you?"

"I don't know, but I wasn't last. And I beat Simpson."

Dad came over to us. "I got worried when you hit the new triple. It looked like you were going to lose it."

"You were worried? I thought I was going down!" I shouted. "But the front end lifted, and I rode it out."

Dad chuckled. "I also noticed that your back tire stopped and spun again after you landed." I looked at Dad and then at John. There was something I wasn't getting here.

"So?"

"When you're airborne and you hit your back brake, it makes your front end drop. If you race the engine, it makes your front end lift," said John.

"Oh," I said, wondering why.

Dad explained. "When you go off a jump, both wheels are spinning. If you put on your back brake, that spinning moves into the motorcycle's frame. So when you hit the back brake, it makes the front end drop."

I remembered hitting the brakes late, after I was in the air. This made the front dip. "Yeah, well, I didn't crash, which is the main thing. I guess I have good luck," I said.

"You have to ride smart and stay lucky. You have to make your own luck." *Here comes another one*, I thought. Dad certainly did give plenty of speeches!

"How do you make your own luck?" I asked.

Dad began to explain. "Suppose you're following another rider and you can't get past him. So you follow him closely for a lap, looking for a chance to pass. If he gets nervous because you're pressuring him, he might fall. Then you're on top of him and you fall too. Bad luck, right?"

"Yeah, right."

"Now suppose you pick a line to follow him that's not directly behind him. He still feels the pressure and falls. But this time you pass right by him and move up a spot. Good luck? Sure, but you made it by being smart. Understand?"

"Yeah, I guess so." He winked at me and

walked off. Dad always talked this way. It was like a riddle or something. I smiled and walked over to my bike. I had to prepare it for the second moto.

I sat on the starting line, warming up my Honda in the far outside gate. My plan was to carry a lot of speed into the first turn. I would pass all the other riders on the far outside. I didn't want to get tangled up in the middle like last time.

The signboard went sideways and I held the throttle open. All the bikes screamed together. The engines and riders were ready to race. The gate moved.

My bike lunged forward, only to come to a sudden stop. The line of riders roared off as my back tire spun. My front tire was wedged under the gate. I had not let the gate drop down, now I was stuck behind it. Instantly, I pulled in the clutch and yanked back on the bars. The gate fell and I was off. This took only two seconds, but I was in last place.

My Honda was ripping across the dirt. Up ahead, the pack was bumping and feeling their way into the first turn. Somebody must have rubbed tires because three bikes went down all at once. As I caught up to them, I went to the outside. Meanwhile, other riders were trying to get around the fallen bikes. Up ahead I saw that John was past the pile-up. In the middle of the pack, one rider seemed to pop up into the air. It was number ten—Steve Simpson. He had ridden right over one of the downed bikes. This tactic moved him up higher on my do-not-like-list.

I rode a smooth line out of the turn and passed two bikes. It felt good. I was proud of myself.

My speed and technique were perfect over the first jump. My landing was smooth and easy. I ripped up the track heading for the next turn. Two riders coasted through the inside of the turn, so I went up high. I hit the gas early, pulling away from the other two bikes. *Yes, two more.*

My throttle was wide open on the straightaway with the brown monster waiting. My blood was pumping hard. It felt as though the excitement of the race was making my entire body shake.

Once again, the brown monster threw me at the sky. With my motor silent, I heard wind whistle around my helmet. It was a brief moment of peace as I waited to drop back down. This time I flew under control, no panic, no problem. As I started to drop, I tapped the rear brake. The front dipped perfectly and I landed solidly. *Thanks for the tip, Dad.*

As I swept around the next turn, I looked ahead. Two riders were directly in front of me. One of them was Simpson. I set my sights on him and got down to business. *Ride smart, ride fast, focus and breathe,* I told myself.

Everything was working perfectly for me on this run. It was the most comfortable I'd ever felt on a motorcycle. I dove into the corners and came out like a pro each time. The jumps passed beneath me without any effort at all. I was in a zone and it felt amazing.

After two laps, I caught up to the rider behind Simpson. We came around to the big tabletop jump nearly side by side. I drifted to the right and followed him off the ramp. Neither of us cleared the jump. Instead, we landed about ten feet short of the ramp. My ankles took the shock and sent me a flash of pain. I ignored the jolt and kept riding hard. We raced across the top of the jump and dropped through the air. Then it was full throttle to the turn.

I came alongside of him as we got to the turn. My right side position put me on the inside of the turn. I was able to come out of it ahead of him. He was now behind me.

Steve was up ahead and there was just one lap left to catch him. Although about ten riders were ahead of us, Simpson was my main focus. Within half a lap I was closing in and looking for a chance to pass. We leaped over the next jump side by side, sharing a glance in midair. With dirt shooting from our tires, we moved to the turn. Steve had the inside, but he only gained a few inches on me. We ripped down the long straight as we headed for the monster. I felt confident that I could out jump him and got ready to fly.

Simpson knew what I was thinking. Just as we approached the big ramp, the slime bucket steered at me. He faked like he was about to crash into me. Then he quickly steered away. This move broke my concentration and I hit my brakes. My launch on the big triple was barely under control and I landed short.

His dirty riding had worked—he definitely slowed me down.

His trick was dangerous. It took all my willpower to avoid thinking about punching his lights out. After the jump, Steve had picked up a few feet on me. I pushed myself just short of crashing trying to catch up to him. Dad's words repeated themselves in my head. "Ride smart and make your own luck."

I went over the small tabletop. My Honda seemed to grunt when I landed beyond the down ramp. Steve put his Yamaha in front of me as we dashed down the hill. My front tire hit his bouncing rear tire. I didn't fall and kept going.

We scrambled back up the hill, engines wailing and tires spinning. I followed him and looked ahead to the upcoming jumps. One double jump followed by another was just what I needed to get past him. Steve drifted wide out of the turn. It was almost too good to be true. He had given me a chance to pass him. I went for it with my throttle wide open.

Then I realized that maybe this was too good to be true. I was right. Suddenly, he moved back to the right to cut me off. I moved over to the left as he passed directly in front of me.

I took the next two jumps in stride, separating myself from Steve a bit. I screamed as I dove into the next turn. "Eat my dirt, Simpson!" I felt so good I thought I would explode. The finish line was just ahead. But Steve wasn't giving up. I could hear him right behind me. He stayed with me over a short tabletop and through some turns.

There was one more turn before the finish. It spun the rider around 180 degrees and had a huge, high bank. The fastest way through was to ride on the base of the bank. That's where I went, but not Steve. He slowed and cut the turn tight on the inside. Instead of holding this line, he moved out wide, heading straight at me.

It looked like he was going to ride right off the track. But he skidded his back wheel so it whacked into my front tire. Then he was back on the gas. Down I went, with rocks from his rear wheel hitting me in the face. I flipped over the side of my bike and landed on my back. Simpson rode off as I quickly jumped to my feet. One kick brought my Honda back to life. I scrambled for the checkered flag as three riders went by me. The race was over, but not for me.

I jumped off my bike and charged Simpson. I was overwhelmed with anger. Three times he had tried to make me crash.

I jumped on his back, knocking him off his bike. I grabbed hold of his helmet, trying to rip it off. A clump of his red hair was stuck in my hand. My right hand punched him in the face, well, actually the helmet. I didn't say anything. I let my fists do the talking.

Steve was big. He fought back hard, landing punches, as well as a helmet head-butt. From his position on his back, though, he was no match for me.

CHAPTER ELEVEN

SEEING RED

"What's going on here?" a man yelled.

I threw a final punch at Simpson as the man grabbed my arm. I got back up and tried to charge him again. Hands reached out of the crowd and pulled us apart.

"He tried to kill me!" I screamed. "You do that again and I'll rip your leg off and beat you with it!" Spit was flying out of my mouth along with the words. I struggled to get loose so I could hit him again.

"I didn't do a thing to you!"

"Three times you tried to make me crash! I'm gonna tear your head off!" I fought my way toward him.

"You touch him again and it'll be your head that comes off!" Steve's father snapped.

"That was a legal block-pass!" Steve yelled at me.

"Legal? You crashed right into me!" I struggled again to break free.

"Jason!" My father shouted, running over. Dad held me back and spoke firmly into my ear. "All right, just calm down for a second." He drew my attention away from Steve. "Keep your mouth shut and pick up your bike." He looked madder than I was—which made me back down.

"He crashed right into me," I replied.

"Just pick up the bike and walk away!" I stared back at him and then pulled my bike off the ground. I was angry at Steve but just as angry at Dad now. He wasn't even standing up for me. I'd hardly even see him for the first ten years of my life. Now, the first chance he gets, he abandons me again.

The crowd parted. I looked straight ahead and walked past them. My father followed.

"This ain't over, kid," snarled Steve's father. I whipped my head around, ready to yell back at him. I never got the chance.

In a flash, Dad was right in the man's face. Dad's eyes drilled into him. "Don't talk to my son like that. Don't even look at my son." Dad spoke forcefully. "It definitely *is* over. Now get out of my way, and keep your mouth shut."

Dad and I kept walking back to our truck. Steve's father was a big guy, standing half a foot taller than Dad. He had a barrel chest and a full size beer gut. But he kept quiet after Dad got in his face.

My anger at Dad disappeared instantly. Suddenly, a sense of happiness and pride rush over my entire body. *That's right. You tell him Dad!* I had made a lot of stupid mistakes in my life. Maybe going after Steve was another one, but Dad stood by my side. I was his son and he wasn't going to let anybody hurt me. I felt safe, protected, and loved—it was a good feeling.

The track sounds swirled around me as I walked back to the truck. The next race was finishing its first lap. Motorcycle engines screamed as the bikes flew by. I slowly calmed down as I made my way to the truck. My breathing and pulse slowed. The noises of the track had a calming effect on me. The rest of the world really didn't care about my anger. They were moving on, and so should I.

"What happened?" John asked.

I spoke. "Simpson crash-passed me. He's not fast enough to pass me clean. He had to cheat and knock me down to get by." Dad and Ann stood nearby and listened.

"How did he do it?" John asked.

"On the last turn before the finish, he skidded into my front wheel. Not only that, but he tried two other times to take me down." I told John about what happened on the triple step-up and the double-double. Then I pulled off my chest protector and jersey.

Nobody said anything. There was tension in the air that I didn't understand. I stood there for a few seconds feeling confused. I walked to the front of the truck and changed into my shorts. I had expected some more support from John. I was waiting for a comment about what a cheat Simpson was. Instead, I was met with silence.

"Three times he tried to make me crash, John." I said again. My brother didn't say anything back. I sensed that he didn't agree with me. I felt myself getting angry again.

"Would you like a bottle of water?" Ann offered.

"No," I snapped.

"Jason, why don't you take a walk and relax for a while. Then we can talk about this," my father suggested.

"Three times," I said as I walked away from the truck. I tried to stay calm as I watched the high school riders.

How many of them race dirty? I wondered. *How many of them got knocked down by a cheater?* My brain kept replaying my race and my father saying, "we'll talk about it." *Was that just another way of saying you're wrong?*

I loved the way that Dad had stood up for me. Still, I didn't understand why he didn't seem to agree that I had been cheated. *How could he side with Steve? And what about John? Why isn't he taking my side?*

More riders went by. My hand throbbed from punching Steve's helmet. I continued to walk slowly around the back of the track. Eventually I came around to the starting area. I continued to watch the riders as they sped around the track.

Three riders had broken away from the rest and were fighting for the lead. Around they went, stretching out their lead and leaving the others behind. They soared high over the big tabletop and ripped through the turns. On their last lap, I watched them come up on the turn where I had crashed. Suddenly, the second-place rider turned tight across the turn just like Steve had done. He cut in front of the leader who had to brake to avoid hitting him. *That's exactly what had happened to me!* I couldn't believe it. I was sure there was going to be a fight.

I watched the bikes come off the track. The winner stopped and took a bottle of water from a friend. The second-place rider rolled right by him without saying a word. I was shocked. *Why didn't that guy fight him?*

"It's called a block-pass," I heard from behind me. I turned to see my father.

"A block-pass?" I repeated. I felt embarrassed that I didn't know this. "So, Steve isn't the only slime who races motorcycles?"

"There are others. It's a legal pass, Jas." I wore a look of confusion on my face. "Most riders don't use it, but it's legal." Dad paused. "I don't care if it is legal, it shouldn't be happening. It's a dirty way to ride—especially for your age group. You had a great race, Jason. Just be proud of that."

"So I can ride clean, but someone can always crash into me?"

"Most of the time they don't crash. The guy getting cut off is forced to brake. Usually they don't fall."

"That's just wrong."

Dad nodded in agreement. "It's not something kids should be doing to each other. We're here to have fun, not knock each other off the track."

I looked at him. "You don't think I should have hit Steve, do you?"

"What do you think?" Dad asked.

"I think he deserved a beating. I passed him clean. I beat him fair and square. Even though he tried to make me crash, I played it fair." I spoke with confidence.

"Whether he deserved it or not is a different question. You asked if you should have hit him, not whether he deserved it. The answer to that question is no. You could have gotten us banned from the track for fighting. That still might happen. And guess what? You fighting Steve didn't change the outcome of the race, did it?"

"No." Suddenly I understood Dad's point. In fact, my fighting had never done anything positive for me, ever. Suddenly, guilt struck me. I realized that my fight could end my racing career. Also, the last thing I wanted to do was ruin racing for Dad and John. To think that my actions might get them kicked off the track had me nervous. I looked over at Dad and spoke. "I'm sorry. I can fix this, Dad. I mean, I can talk to—"

"Let's just see what happens." With that, he gave me a hug. "Maybe you're playing the wrong sport, Jason. You should look into boxing." He laughed at his joke.

I looked down and flexed my throbbing hand. "I like racing way better than boxing."

"Let's go have some lunch," Dad said. We walked back to the truck. As we approached, fear rose in my throat. Standing by the driver's door was Steve's father and Mr. Ford, the track owner.

When we approached the truck, Mr. Ford wasted no time. He spoke to Dad. "Mr. Simpson tells me your son attacked his boy. I want to hear your side of the story." Mr. Ford was about as tall as my father. He was older, but still thickly muscled.

"I see," said my father. "And did he tell you why my son did that?"

"Yes. Steven block-passed your son and your son got angry."

"That's not all he was angry about, Mr. Ford. Steven," Dad pointed at him, "tried to take Jason out twice *before* he crash-passed."

When Dad used my phrase, I knew he was still on my side. He was sticking up for me again. This support was something I had thought was missing from my life. Even if he punished me, Dad would be there for me when I needed him.

Mr. Simpson shot a look of surprise at Steve. "Is this true?" he asked.

"Well," Steve started.

My father cut short Steve's words. "Think about it for a second. We want the truth here. Before you answer, remember, hundreds of people were watching you race."

"Are you calling my son a liar?" Mr. Simpson took a step toward Dad.

"He didn't say anything yet." Dad drilled his hard look into Mr. Simpson's face. Everyone looked at Steve.

"There was a rock in the way so I had to go around it." Steve didn't look up as he spoke.

"When you suddenly cut over, you were trying to avoid a rock?"

"Yeah, that's right." Steve's voice sounded more confident.

"If Jason had done this, would you have thought he was looking for a crash?"

I moved over to my father's side. It made me feel stronger, like we were together.

"Yeah, maybe," Steve said. The adults exchanged glances and Dad continued.

"Tell us what happened just before the double-double. I saw you move over and then suddenly cut back, barely missing Jason's front tire."

"Umm, I was going to take the outside line and then I changed my mind."

"You knew Jason was right behind you, right?" Dad continued, pressing him.

"Yeah."

"If you were Jason, would you have been upset?" The way Dad spoke, calmly, was working.

"Yes, I mean, I don't know."

"After you tried to take him down again, can you understand why he was angry?"

"He jumped me!" Steve screamed out in frustration.

"We know that and now Jason knows he was wrong. Still, you have a responsibility to race in a way that doesn't harm other riders. Isn't that right, Mr. Ford?" Dad looked over at the owner of the track.

"Yes, that's right. We don't want anybody hurt on the track or off it. But I don't allow fighting. The rule is one fight and you're out." I began to get nervous. If we couldn't race anymore . . . "You both should have known better," Mr. Ford said.

"My son Jason is new to the sport, and the track. He didn't know about the no-fighting rule. He also didn't know that Steve was trying to put a block-pass on him. He thought that he was just trying to knock him over. I've spoken to him about this and it won't happen again."

Mr. Ford looked at him and then at me. I could tell he was really thinking about what to do. My stomach tightened up as I thought again about not racing anymore.

"I don't do usually this, but I'm going to give you another chance." *Yes! Way to go Dad!*

Mr. Ford looked at me and waved his pointy finger. "But I don't want any more fighting! One more and you're gone."

"Yes, sir. Never again. I apologize."

Then he looked over at Steve. "And I don't want to see you trying to make other riders crash."

"Yes, sir, I understand."

"If this happens again, both families will be banned from the track." He gave a tough stare to each of us and walked away. I felt happy as I looked at Steve. He stared back like he wanted to injure me. Mr. Simpson had a very disappointed look on his face as well. I turned away to hide my smile and followed Dad back to the truck.

That night, rain blew against the side of the house. I wrapped myself tighter in the thin cotton sheet. It wasn't the rain that kept me awake though, it was my racing memories.

The race track flashed in my mind every time I closed my eyes. In my head, I was racing toward the brown monster, then dropping from the sky! A moment later, Steve's bike was spraying dirt in my face. Then, there was the excitement of finishing before Steve in the first moto. My heart jumped as I replayed these memories. Mixed in with this was the fight, and the confrontation with the Simpson family.

There was no way I could sleep. "John, are you awake?" I whispered. There was silence. I shook the bunk-bed. A "what" drifted up to me. "I can't sleep."

"Try harder," John mumbled.

"How can you sleep after racing today?"

"I just close my eyes and stop talking. You should try it."

"I keep seeing the track in my mind, you know?"

"Hmmm."

"And Steve, that was so cool when I beat him in the first moto. It was like, I don't know—it was the best."

That comment was followed by a few seconds of silence. Then I could hear John sit up in his bed. "Why did you jump on his back, Jas?"

"I don't know. I was angry." I paused. "I guess—I let the anger take control of me, you know?"

"You don't beat someone up because he cut you off. You're lucky we didn't get kicked out of there for good."

"I know. Sometimes, I just get angry and let myself go. I've actually been a lot better since I got here."

"Geez," John laughed. "What were you like in California—a serial killer?"

"Shut up," I laughed. Then I got serious.

"Sometimes I just open the box and start punching." I shared my deepest secret with John.

"What box?"

"My bad box. I have this imaginary box inside of my chest. I've had it there since I was little. You know, it's hard growing up without a father around, John." He had a Mom *and* a Dad all those years. I didn't.

"I bet," he said, "that would really suck."

"Anyway, it made me really angry for a long time. I'm just now getting over it. When someone does something that angers me, I put that anger in the box. Then when it gets too full, I open the box. All the bad stuff comes flying out." It felt strange talking about this. I had never told anyone this stuff before. Actually, I had never really thought about it before.

"Wouldn't it be better to just forget it? To keep the anger inside of your box without letting it out?"

"Yeah, but it's not that easy. Like today, when Steve made me crash. The box was overflowing and I just had to fight. I couldn't help myself." More rain hit the window. "But I have another box, on the other side of my chest." I didn't know if I should tell John more. He might think I was crazy. I kept talking anyway.

"What do you keep in that one, something to eat?" John laughed at his own joke.

"No, stupid." I reached over and hit him with the pillow. "I put good things in this one. Things like when I finished ahead of Simpson in the first moto. The trouble is that the good stuff leaks out through a drain after a while."

"Why don't you hook up a drain to the bad box? You can put a drain tube that runs from your bad box to your bladder. Then when you go to the bathroom you can get rid of the bad stuff." John laughed again.

This time I joined him. "Now that's a great idea! You're pretty smart for a short kid with a tiny brain."

"Yeah, I get that way when people won't let me sleep." I jumped down from the top bunk. "Where are you going?" John asked.

"To the bathroom, I have a few people to get out of my system."

CHAPTER TWELVE

BELLY UP IN THE RIVER

"I want you to work on John's old bike," Dad told me at breakfast. "You've been riding it here for a month, it's time to rebuild." Dad got up and poured himself another cup of coffee. He reached into his pocket and handed me two hundred-dollar bills. "Take this, and get what you need to make this thing run like new. I expect some change, too."

I took the money and smiled. "You'll get some. Don't worry. When you sell this thing, you should get good value. It rides well and once I rebuild the engine—"

Dad cut me off. "I'm not selling it."

"You're keeping both bikes?"

"No, when you leave, the bike goes with you. It'll meet you in California a few days after you get home."

"Are you serious?" I nearly tackled Dad to give

him a hug. "That is the greatest thing that I've ever heard!" *I own a motorcycle! When I get home, I can keep riding!* "Thank you, thank you, thank you! This is the most amazing—"

"Just make sure you fix it up right," Dad said, with a big smile. John walked into the room. "John, help your brother with his bike today. Make sure you keep everything organized when you rebuild the engine."

"Did you tell him?" John asked, excited.

Dad smiled. "Yup."

"It's a great bike," John said.

It was nice to see how excited John was for me. He really wanted me to have that bike. "This is awesome," I said. "Let's go, John. No time for breakfast, we've got to rebuild this engine!"

As John and I left the house, I was floating on air. I turned toward him. "Do you know how to do all this?"

"Pretty much. If we were pro riders, we'd have mechanics who would work on our bikes."

"That would be so awesome. I want to be a pro someday," I said.

"Yeah, me too. Maybe we can. We both have bikes now. We can practice all the time—motocross brothers, right?"

I nodded my head and we walked toward the barn.

"Maybe you'll come back next summer," John

said as we stepped into the barn. "It would be cool if you did. I mean, if you wanted to."

I'd never thought about this, but it sounded like a great idea. "Definitely—if your Mom wants me here and—"

"You're family, man!" John said. "We're stuck with you whether we like it or not."

I smiled. "Yeah, I'll be back next summer for sure."

We walked into the barn and John held open the manual. During the next few hours, we slowly took the bike apart. By lunchtime, the bike was in about a hundred pieces. There were a few parts we needed to replace but, overall, the engine looked good.

We left the barn and headed for the motocross store by the gas station. As we neared the gas station, I noticed a man walking to his white car. He had a sloppy handful of papers he was stuffing into his pocket. As he pulled his hand out, one piece was carried off by the wind. It skipped across the pavement and folded itself around a weed by the road. I kept my eye on it and then I picked it up. It was a twenty-dollar bill!

I held it in the air as I looked for the white car. A second later, I saw it turning and driving away from us. I tried to wave him down, but he was long gone. This was my lucky day.

"Lunch is on me brother," I said with a smile. "Let's pick up the supplies after we eat." We grabbed our bikes and pedaled across the road to Bob's Burgers.

"Is this for here or to go?" the woman asked. I recognized her from my first day.

"To go," John answered for us.

"Any more problems with the fry machine?" I asked her.

"Not since the last time you were here," she grinned. "Have a nice day, boys." She handed us two bags filled with burgers, fries, and milkshakes.

"Why don't we eat here?" I asked, as we got on our bikes.

"I want to eat by the river. Follow me." We crossed over the highway and then turned down a dirt road. The road split the tall, green corn fields. We took a left onto a smaller road. Grass and weeds grew up between the two tracks. It twisted back and forth going gradually down hill. We pedaled past an old empty farmhouse and barn. Boards were nailed over the barn's doors.

My fries are going to be soggy, I thought as I coasted down hill. The walls of corn suddenly ended and I saw a wide stream. The water moved along and disappeared around a tight bend. John dropped his bike by the edge of the water.

"What do you think?" John asked.

"I think my food is cold."

"Leave it out in the sun, that'll warm it up." I gave him a dirty look. "Isn't this great? Look how fast the water is flowing."

"Yeah, it is, actually." I quit being annoyed and tried to enjoy the river. I sat under the shade of one of the few trees and ate. The early afternoon sun was really cooking us. Only the water and the flies could be heard over our chewing.

After packing the wrappers into his bag, John announced, "I'm going in the water." I took off my shirt and sneakers and followed him in. It was colder than I had expected. I carefully moved my way across the rocky bottom.

"Wow! Who turned on the cold water?"

"It feels good doesn't it?" John said, treading water in the middle of the river.

The water was up to my shorts. "Once you're in." A few strokes brought us out into the current. We floated on our backs with our arms stretched out. I kept my ears underwater to stay afloat. I heard my breathing echo in my head. The world seemed to stop.

I soon realized that I was moving downstream pretty quick. The current had moved us along and the bottom suddenly dropped away. We were floating around a turn, about to be pushed against the high rocky wall.

"Watch out for the rock!" I yelled to John. He turned around just in time to reach out for it. I touched it a second later. The water pushed us against a huge rock sticking out of the bank. I felt the current trying to pull my legs under the rock.

"Check this out," John said. He floated on his back with his feet against the side of the rock. I followed his example as water moved beneath me. It was like standing sideways. Water smacked against my back and I closed my eyes to the sun. A minute later, a big, black cloud passed over us. I looked up at the wall of dirt and rock. The wind picked up a bit as well.

"John, look at that." I pointed to an opening in the rocks, a few feet above us.

"Cool, it's like a cave." We climbed onto the rock for a closer look.

The opening was about the size of two garbage cans. Without too much trouble, I climbed inside. It went back about eight feet and then the passage became narrow. If I went on my hands and knees, my back hit the top.

"What's in there?" John asked.

"Come in and check this out!"

"Wait, uh-oh, Jas," John pointed toward the sky. I peeked my head out of the cave and looked. "We better get home fast." John said. The sky was filled with black storm clouds.

"So, no big deal, we'll get wet."

"Forget wet, we could get dead. Those are tornado clouds." He leaped off the rock into the river, swimming hard for the shore. I followed him, looking up in fear at the sky above us. The ugly black clouds seemed to touch the ground. They were rolling toward us fast. The breeze was getting stronger, with gusts throwing dirt. A taste of fear formed in my mouth.

We climbed out of the water. I ran after John as fast as my bare feet could carry me. It felt like I was stepping on knives, as rocks and weeds smacked my feet. The wind whipped around from every direction. I had never seen weather like this in my life. The sun was completely blocked and we couldn't see more than a hundred feet. The wind was spitting dirt and dust right at us.

At first, John tried to follow a small path along the stream. As the storm got closer, though, he led me through thick weeds toward our bikes. Our shirts were nowhere to be found, but our sneakers had blown into the weeds. We quickly put them on.

"We can't make it home!" John yelled in my ear. "The storm is in the way!"

"Let's go to the old farm house!" John nodded and tried to pedal. Hail suddenly began to fall, hitting us like small stones. Then the rain came down in buckets. The wind was getting stronger by the second. I could hardly keep my eyes open with so much dirt in the air. I gave up on the bike and ran past John with my arm guarding my eyes. Corn stalks were flying everywhere. With my head down, I leaned into the wind and pushed forward. We had to make it to the house and find shelter, right now! I felt John pulling at my arm.

His mouth was moving but I couldn't hear him

over the wind. I followed his pointing arm forward. In the distance, I could see the top of the barn. And then it wasn't there—it was gone! The roof slowly lifted off the top. Then it crumbled apart and disappeared into the swirling mix of rain and dirt.

John pulled my arm in the other direction. With wind at our backs, we ran at full speed down to the river. As we got to the sand, a flying corn stalk hit John in the head. He landed face first and cut his lip pretty bad. I grabbed his arm and helped him up. Blood dripped off his cut lip. He pointed down stream. I looked at him, not understanding. He pointed again as he got to his feet.

We ran along the bank as the wind continued to pick up speed. We could now see the tornado and it wasn't far from us. We were about to be sucked up into it. The wind seemed to push us from all directions at the same time. We could barely see. *This is the end*, I thought. *We're going to die. Any second the wind is going to lift us into the sky. Then the gust will drive us against the ground and smash us like tomatoes.* As John pulled me toward the river, I understood his plan—the cave!

We moved quickly, carried by our fear. I was coughing and swallowing water as we fought our way across. Finally, we made it to the far bank and the rock slab. I reached out for the big rock and scrambled up into the cave.

I looked back at John to see his hand slipping

down the rock. Water flowed over his sinking head. I lunged for his hand and pulled him up with everything I had. The current was dragging him under the rock. His other hand touched the rock but couldn't find a hold. He looked up at me from two inches below the swirling water. I saw his eyes and mouth, wishing for air.

I reached down into the water and closed my fingers around his hair. I pulled him up and away from the rock. John's face broke the surface inches away from mine. His mouth was open, coughing, and breathing.

"Push away from the rock!" I yelled in his face, still pulling him. He wiggled his way up a few inches. I moved my grip to his elbow. Then I got my feet beneath me and could pull harder. John moved up the rock a little higher. I pulled him out of the water by his shorts and into the cave. We lay there catching our breath, coughing, and resting.

"Move all the way in!" John yelled.

We moved deep into the cave so that the wind barely touched us. We could hear it screaming and howling. Rain and hail was thrown against our feet and legs. "It's cold," John said. I had noticed this too. The air temperature had dropped at least twenty degrees.

"What's that noise?" Outside, the wind got louder. It sounded like a freight train was passing by.

"I think that's the sound of a tornado," John

said. I could barely hear him. I pulled my feet in a little closer. It felt like a vacuum cleaner was trying to pull us out of the cave.

"Hang on to something," I yelled. The pull got stronger and we pushed against the cave walls to fight the force. I closed my eyes and pushed, driving my back against the rocky wall. After a minute, the pull stopped and the roar died down.

"The wind is slowing down. I don't feel the rain on my feet anymore." We both tried to look out.

"I'm ready to get out of here," I said. I slowly wiggled out. My legs reached down for the big rock and then for the river. I saw that the sky was a lighter shade of gray. I stood up and looked around. "John."

"What?"

"I don't believe it," I said.

"What?" he said crawling out.

"The water's gone."

"What?"

"Look, the water in the river is gone." I was shocked. In front of us lay a wet riverbed with barely any water. A few logs and old tires were scattered among the wet rocks. "Where did it go?"

"I don't know. Let's just go home." We climbed down to the riverbed. The mud was slick and clung to our shoes. The water from upstream began making its way between the rocks, refilling the river.

"So, where did the water go?" I asked again as we walked along the bank.

"Up, I guess."

"Up where?"

"The storm sucked it up. I saw this on TV once. Tornadoes can suck ponds dry, rivers too. That must have been the pulling thing we felt."

"Like it rained up?"

"Yeah, I guess so." I looked back at the river. It was flowing again now, but much slower and with less water. We turned up the path to the old house.

Our bikes were gone. The barn was gone. That gave us a spooky feeling. If we had hid in it, we would probably been gone, too. We found one of the bikes when we turned onto the dirt road. It was all bent and smashed.

"You know, that could have been us." I put my hand on John's shoulder as we stared down at the bike.

"I know." He looked at me. His eyes were filled with tears. "Thanks for pulling me onto the rock."

"No problem, brother."

I felt a bond with John like no other bond I had ever experienced. I had a brother for life.

CHAPTER THIRTEEN

JASON'S GOOD

The next four weeks were awesome. I continued to race and even managed to finish in the top five
three times. I was improving more every day. John
and I eventually finished rebuilding my engine. My bike
was riding better than ever. After having spent over
two months in Iowa, I had learned a lot. I'd changed a
lot, too. I was excited to show my mother the *new*
and improved Jason. I was also excited to show off
my skills on the track.

A few days before I would be flying home, I
heard the phone ring. *That's gotta be Mom.* I heard
Ann pick up the phone and say hello.

I walked faster, excited to speak to her. Over
the past few months, I truly began to appreciate my
mother. When I got back home, I knew that things
would change between the two of us. I was done
giving her such a hard time. If she wanted, I'd even

go to a NASCAR race with her and George!

I grabbed the phone from Ann. "Hi, Mom."

"How's it going?" Her voice was cheerful.

"Good, I was just packing the truck for tomorrow's race."

"Your last race, huh? Don't get hurt! Did you get the airplane ticket I sent?"

"Yup, it came today."

"Good. Your father told me that he's giving you that motorcycle. That was really nice of him. I'm—uh, really excited to watch you race it."

"Really?" I asked, with excitement.

"Your father says that you were born to do this. So I guess I might as well be a fan, right?"

I smiled from ear to ear. "Thanks, Mom."

"George will pick you up at the airport on Tuesday. And I don't want to hear any arguments. I can't get you because—"

I cut her off. "Sounds fine. It'll be good to see George." I said.

Mom gave a confused laugh. "Sure," she said.

The next morning, dew soaked my sneakers in the grass at the racetrack parking field. A few minutes later, John and I passed by Steve Simpson. *Here we go.*

"Hey, it's the loser brothers," he shouted.

"That's funny, Steve. But we both beat you badly the last time we raced. Why don't you save your dad's money and just watch from behind the fence?" It was kind of fun to tease Steve. Especially since I beat him fairly consistently now.

"I'm going to beat you bad today, Jason. At least your little brother knows how to ride. You can barely even stay on your bike. Loser! You'll be eating dirt all day." He paused, pointing to his bike. "I've got a new motor and I went to motocross camp last week. And there's another reason I'll beat you— because you're a big-mouth loser."

Steve was crossing the line by calling me a loser again and again. My bad box was almost filled up. I wanted to run over and hit him, but I forced myself to hold back. I had been practicing controlling my temper all summer long. Steve wasn't making that easy on me—that much was for sure.

"You can go to camp from now until Christmas," I said. "It's not going to make a difference. You haven't got what it takes, Stevie." I smiled but it wasn't a nice one. "Daddy can't buy you brains or skills." He turned and narrowed his eyes at me.

"Why don't you put some money where your big mouth is, loser? Or are you just all mouth?"

I looked around to see if my father was close. If he knew I had bet on the race, he wouldn't be happy. He was a few hundred yards away. So I shouted to Steve. "How much?"

"One hundred bucks says I finish before you." Steve sounded confident.

"You're on," I said casually, not backing down an inch. "And when you lose, you better pay up."

As he walked off, John asked, "Do you even have a hundred dollars?"

"Almost, I have seventy-five. You have twenty-five, right little brother?"

"You better win, you idiot."

"No problem." I wasn't quite as confident as I made it sound. I had beaten Steve more than half the time, but only a few seconds. *What if his new motor really is fast? What if he got better at motocross camp? A hundred dollars is a lot of money.*

As John and I sat on our bikes at the starting area, I looked around. Memories of my first race came back to me. Eight weeks ago, I thought all I had to do to win was take chances. And all I had to do to be liked was to brag and be crazy. It wasn't like that anymore. I was controlled and confident, but not cocky.

John interrupted my thoughts. "You know that today's race is the power sports vehicle race. The winner gets a huge trophy. Plus, if you win, you get a hundred bucks!" I thought about all the cool stuff I could get with a hundred dollars. *Maybe a new helmet and some new gloves.* I thought about the giant trophy. It made my throttle hand twitch.

I turned back toward John. "Let's try to take first and second place today. My last race of the season, you know. Besides, you could use another second place trophy!"

John held up one finger and pointed to himself. I shook my head no and did the same. I glanced over at Steve. As I stared at him, I wished I hadn't made that bet. Now, with the money on the line, it could get ugly. Steve was going to be after me in both motos.

The trackman waved us to the starting gates. A minute later, I was staring at the gate in front of my tire. Suddenly, it moved. I released the clutch lever and snapped the throttle wide open. My Honda leaped forward. I kicked it up a gear a second later. My sights were set on the inside of the first turn. Motorcycles closed in around me.

Side by side with five other riders, I leaped into the air. We fought for position going into the next turn. The other bikes forced me into a high, outside line. It was the long way around, but I went in fast. I dragged the front brake and leaned forward. I was riding the perfect race. I held my speed and came out fast, passing two riders. Looking at the brown monster, I realized I was in first place!

My body shook at the thought of being in the lead. I had only dreamed of this moment. But could I hold on for the rest of the race? Self-doubt crept up my throat. I quickly stuffed it into my bad box and slammed the lid closed. *Stay focused*, I told myself.

The long straight was gone in a blur of speed and noise. I hit the monster faster than ever before, soaring up high. A quick look over my shoulder showed me John was right behind. Steve was in fourth place.

I landed perfectly on the down ramp beyond the third step. This carried me into the long sweeper. I picked my line and powered around it. Nobody was in front of me spraying dirt up into my face or blocking my line.

The track smoothed out. Everything clicked into place. John was still behind me when I peeked over my shoulder. The last lap began and I was still in the lead. Steve was now on John's rear tire, looking for a chance to pass.

A moment later, the checkered flag flashed. I crossed the finish line in first place. I had won the first moto! Excitement, pride, happiness, and satisfaction hit me at once. I allowed myself one loud "yes!" Then I got under control again.

When I came off the track I pretended that it was no big deal. Inside of me, fireworks were going off.

"Great ride, Jason!" my father said.

"Thanks," I said, returning a big smile. He was proud of me.

"Unbelievable race!" John said holding out his fist.

I tapped it with my fist as Steve went past us without a word. Our bet still hung in our minds: The next moto would decide the final outcome.

As the winner, I had first pick of the starting

gates for the second moto. John and I grabbed the two gates in the middle. Steve lined up next to John. My pre-race jitters were higher than usual. I checked over the bike once again. Everything looked good.

I looked over at Steve. He was staring at me. I remembered the time he crash-passed me. I hoped our bet wouldn't push him to do something stupid like that again. The signboard suddenly turned sideways and I got ready to race.

My Honda lunged forward with the other bikes. I got a good jump out of the gate. We came to the first turn, one, two, and three: John, Steve, and me. We popped over the tabletop jump. I rode high around the next turn while John and Steve stayed low. They came out first, but I quickly caught up to them.

We raced down the straight to the brown monster. Pictures of my near crash from months ago flashed in my mind. The flagman in his tower chair watched me fly past him.

Steve slowed at the last second and landed ten feet shorter than I did. I was right alongside of him as we entered the big sweeper. We ripped around the turn side by side. Then we leaped over the next jump together and skipped down the long hill. The braking bumps almost bucked me off, but I held on. As we scrambled back uphill, Steve pulled ahead of me. Looking past him, I saw that John was stretching out his lead.

By the third lap, I knew I had to do something

to get past him. Steve was riding fast and not making mistakes. I decided to make my move on the monster. We scrambled out of the high turn and tore down the straight. Steve flew down the right side of the track and I went down the center. The monster launched us up into the sky. I looked out and saw that John had just lapped one of the slower riders.

I landed with a thump a few feet past Steve. The excitement and satisfaction of the pass buzzed inside of me. *Hang on, concentrate, and don't let him pass*, I told myself. *One more lap and you have him*. I caught up to the lapped rider on the long down-hill. I thought he was going to stay wide and let me by on the inside. I was braking hard in the bumps when he changed his mind and cut me off. I was forced to follow him slowly through the inside of the turn. Mean-while, Steve whipped right past us. I scrambled uphill, trying to stay focused on catching him.

A second lapped rider slowed Steve up ahead. I moved right behind him. As we turned, I went wide. Steve stayed tight inside. We bobbed in and out when, suddenly, a rider ahead was thrown from his bike. His motorcycle flipped wildly right into Steve's path.

I saw Steve nearly go over the handlebars as I went by. He managed to stay on it, but he lost some ground. *If I stay on two wheels, the race is mine.* I spotted John up ahead as I sailed over the big table-top. I turned onto the long straight away in front of the brown monster. I flew down the track with second place in my mind. But as I was about to launch, I noticed that something was wrong.

The flagman had jumped out of his chair. He was running onto the track in the direction of the landing ramp. *John's up there.* I was able to grab some brake before getting into the air. I flew high enough to see the flagman on the track waving at me.

I landed on the second step and steered to the far left. As I rose onto the third step, I saw John lying face down. Another rider was also down nearby. It was obvious that they had crashed. My stomach dropped. I rolled by, watching John carefully.

He moved slowly, trying to get up. *He's okay,* I thought. *Keep going and the win is yours. He's moving around. He's okay!* I noticed the flagman helping the other rider off the track. He wasn't doing his job, which was to warn approaching riders. Steve and the other racers would be coming over that big triple soon. They couldn't see what was happening on top of the jump. I visualized a motorcycle dropping out of the sky and landing on John.

Instantly, I dipped my bars, and spun away from the finish line. I headed back to the top of the jump where the other racers could see me. I came to a stop on top of the third step.

From my position, I saw a rider approaching halfway down the straight. I waved my arm wildly, letting him know that my brother had fallen up ahead. The rider changed direction and avoided landing on

John. At this point, I had given up winning the race—or taking Steve's hundred dollars. Protecting John was more important.

John stood up next to his motorcycle. The flagman helped him on to some grass just off the track. John was safe. Just then, I looked back and saw a bike, number ten, coming down the straight. My race wasn't over yet.

I dipped my bars to spin around. Steve disappeared below the brown monster heading right at me. He jumped right over me as I coasted off the track down hill. As I rolled, I kicked the starter. The motor sprang to life. In front of me, I could see that Steve was halfway around the sweeper. He was about thirty feet ahead of me.

My Honda skipped down that hill like never before. I was going so fast that my tires seemed to just bounce off the bumps. I came into the turn hot, on the far outside. I nailed the gas and rocketed up the hill. Steve was taking it easy, thinking that he'd easily won the race. When I appeared alongside him, he almost lost control.

He had a better position on the next turn so I couldn't get past him. We headed for the big tabletop at full throttle. I launched off the ramp. I went to the throttle while airborne, bringing my front up for a perfect landing. I was right next to Steve. I beat him to the next turn, but I had too much speed. Steve grabbed the inside line and pulled ahead of me again.

I chased him, only half a bike length behind. Once more he grabbed the inside line and held on to the lead. The high turn before the finish line was coming up. There was a rider in front of us who I saw cross the finish line. Steve and I were racing for second place, pride, and a hundred dollars.

What is he going to do? Cut through the inside and block me out, or go wide? I didn't wait to find out. I drifted left. That's when he moved to cut me off. I backed off the gas for half a second. He cut past my front wheel, and I charged for the finish. Steve scrambled to get himself pointed in the right direction. He was counting on taking me out. He hadn't planned on me dodging him. We both got on our motors and made them scream. I crossed the line half a wheel in front of him. I pumped my arm in the air.

Nobody was at the gate to greet me. For a moment, I was disappointed. Then I saw the ambulance and remembered John. I ran as fast as I could to the back of the ambulance. John and the other kid sat there while one of the paramedics checked him.

"Are you all right?" I asked.

"Yeah, I'm fine. Just a little messed up." John smiled.

"What happened on the triple?"

"That slow rider cut into my line as I landed. He hit my front tire. I'm okay, really."

My father came from behind me and put his hand on my shoulder. "I saw what you did, Jason."

He smiled a proud smile. He realized that my efforts to protect John cost me first place. "I know how much you wanted to win that race." He raised his eyebrows telling me he knew about the bet. "You were willing to give that up to protect your brother. That was brave."

Ann came over and gave me a hug next. "Thank you. Jason. That was amazing."

Finally, it was John's turn. "It's good to know you've got my back, bro. Thanks." My good box was full from the race. I was wearing a smile that wrapped all the way around my head. I never thought that it would feel so good to do something good.

"I'm going down to get my trophy." I walked to the office slowly. My final race in Iowa turned out to be my best race. I was starting to see a real future for me in this sport.

In the middle of these thoughts, I saw the small second place trophy. "Awesome," I whispered. I happily accepted it and walked back to the truck. On the way, I passed by Steve's trailer. He walked over to me with a fat bunch of bills in his hand.

"Here." He held it out to me. It must have been all singles. *Maybe it isn't his father's money. Maybe he had saved it up himself.*

"You tried to take me out in that last turn," I said. He had a sad look. He was no longer a threat or a challenge. Despite his dirty tricks, and going to racing camp, he couldn't beat me. I didn't feel like I had won a great victory over him, though. I actually felt bad for him. I checked my bad box. It was gone. The box, the drain, the bad feelings—they were all gone.

"I know it wasn't right, but I wanted to win. I'm sorry." Steve handed me the money, "Take it. You won it fair." I looked at the money.

"Remember what you said about me being a loser?" I asked.

"Yeah."

"I'll give you a hundred bucks to take it back." A small smile slowly lit up his face.

"That's a deal. You're not a loser, Jason." I smiled and handed him his money back. My good box got a little bigger.

The screen door to his camper slammed. Steve's father stood there. "Is he making trouble again, Steven?"

"No, Dad, Jason's good."

TEST YOURSELF...ARE YOU A PROFESSIONAL READER?

Chapter 1: No Escape

What goes on at the Jensen Dairy Farm?

When Jason returns home from watching the races, what is sitting on top of the kitchen table?

When was the last time Jason had been to Iowa? What happened on that trip?

ESSAY

How does Jason feel about his father? From what you know about Jason and his family, do you think Jason going to Iowa is a good idea? Explain your answer.

Chapter 2: Iowa

What does Jason do at Bob's Burgers that makes John laugh?

What does Jason discover while looking around John's bedroom?

What is Jason counting as he sits by the side of the road?

ESSAY

Jason feels upset and overwhelmed in the barn with his half-brother. What sets him off? If you were in Jason's shoes, would you react in a similar way? Explain your answer.

Chapter 3: Making a Splash

What dangerous stunt does Jason perform? What lie does Jason tell about the noise against the house?

How does Jason's father punish him for the lies he has told?

What is the difference between the ways that Jason's father and mother punish him?

ESSAY

Why do you think Jason lies? When his father calls him out on these lies, what is Jason's reaction? Have you ever been caught in a lie, or caught someone you know in a lie? Describe the situation.

Chapter 4: The Ride

At the beginning of this chapter, Jason is lying in bed unable to sleep. What question does he ask John after he wakes him up? What is John's answer?

Why did Jason think that the motorcycle was broken before John convinced him otherwise?

What does John compare a motorcycle to so that Jason understands how to ride better?

ESSAY

Describe what you learned about how a motorcycle works. Try to use three of following terms in your answer: brake, choke, throttle, neutral, and gear box.

Chapter 5: My First Race

What word does Jason use four times to get his mother to agree to let him race motocross?

What does Jason do when Steve Simpson laughs at him, and says "last is last, loser?" Is this reaction abnormal for Jason?

What does Dad tell John and Jason at the end of this chapter that gets them excited?

ESSAY

"I no longer resented John for being the one who grew up with Dad. I accepted our situation for what it was—imperfect." What does this quote mean? Do you think accepting an imperfect situation is a good thing to do? Explain your answer.

Chapter 6: Mega-Fight

What does Jason do to provoke Steve Simpson at Mega-Mart?

How does Jason fight back when Steve Simpson grabs him by the shirt and looks ready to punch him?

Why do the security guards tackle Steve Simpson as he runs out of the store?

ESSAY

After the events that take place in Mega-Mart, Jason and Steve Simpson are officially enemies. Do you think Jason is right to provoke Steve after he had been hurt by him at the track? What do you think will happen next?

Chapter 7: Mouse Catch

What does Jason throw to John that freaks him out?

Who does Jason think is his number one fan? What regret does he have regarding this person?

What element of motocross racing is John helping Jason master on their basic backyard track?

ESSAY

In this chapter, Jason says that he has changed since coming to Iowa. How has he changed? Explain your answer using details from the first 7 chapters.

Chapter 8: Why, Dad?

When Jason realizes that he is actually driving a real tractor, which two people come to his mind right away?

In this chapter, Jason's father makes him "stop the tractor" at one point. Why?

What is Jason's father's explanation for why he left Jason and his mother?

ESSAY

The reasons behind two people getting divorced are never simple. Jason's father gives Jason many reasons why things didn't work out between him and Jason's mother. Do you know anybody that has gotten a divorce? Why are divorces so difficult on families?

Chapter 9: Jumps

Describe the big-triple jump.

What kind of motorcycle does Steve Simpson ride?

"My brain said slow down, and stay under control. But my emotions wouldn't let me hear it." Explain this quote, as it relates to Jason and Steve Simpson.

ESSAY

Practice makes perfect is a common expression. In this chapter, through practice, Jason begins making improvements out on the track. Do you think this saying only applies to sports? Have you ever practiced hard and improved at something? Explain.

Chapter 10: Block-Pass

Dad tells Jason, "You have to make your own luck." What does this mean?

What rider rolled right over one of the fallen bikes?

What causes Jason to fall during the race?

ESSAY

Why does Jason attack Steve Simpson? What do you think would have been a better way for Jason to handle the situation without fighting?

Chapter 11: Seeing Red

Why does Jason get angry at Dad when he tells Jason to keep his mouth shut and pick up his bike?

What does Jason notice while he is watching the high school-aged motocross racers?

Who is Mr. Ford? Why is he standing next to Dad's truck waiting to talk to Jason?

ESSAY

There is some discussion in this chapter about whether or not Steve deserves to get jumped. Jason's father says, "Whether he deserved it or not is a different question, Jas. You asked if you should have hit him, not whether he deserved it. The answer to that question is no." What do you think he means by that?

Chapter 12: Belly Up in the River

What gift does Dad give Jason in this chapter?

Describe the cave that John and Jason hide in during the storm.

What happens to the river?

ESSAY

Do you think a river can really be sucked dry by a tornado? Go online and see if you can find any information about river's being sucked dry by tornados. Describe what you found out.

Chapter 13: Jason's Good

At the end of their phone conversation, Jason's mother gives a "confused laugh." Why do you think she is confused?

Why does Jason feel bad about taking the bet with Steve?

What does Jason do when he realizes that John has fallen and might be injured by an incoming motorcycle?

ESSAY

After reading this book, in what ways do you think you and Jason are similar? Different? Do you think Jason had *really* changed? Why or why not?